Praise for Elizabeth Partridge's

DOGTAG
SUMMER

★ "Powerful historical fiction." —*Publishers Weekly*, starred review

"Creative and winsome . . . Tracy's escapades help to
build this poignant coming-of-age into a story that resonates
with pain and a hard-fought resolution." —*Booklist*

"Partridge . . . succeeds in incorporating solid historical research
into a moving story, using the dogtag, symbol of a most
unpopular war, as an instrument of catharsis, bringing truth
to light and allowing healing and human connection." —*SLJ*

"Well-written and thoughtful." —*New York Journal of Books*

"Impressive. . . . A strong yet gentle read." —*Kirkus Reviews*

"Tracy's backstory is a dramatic one." —*BCCB*

DOGTAG
SUMMER

Elizabeth Partridge

BLOOMSBURY

NEW YORK BERLIN LONDON SYDNEY

For Sydney Feeney

First published in the United States of America in March 2011
by Bloomsbury Books for Young Readers
Paperback edition published in May 2012
www.bloomsburykids.com

For information about permission to reproduce selections from this book, write to
Permissions, Bloomsbury BFYR, 175 Fifth Avenue, New York, New York 10010

The Library of Congress has cataloged the hardcover edition as follows:
Partridge, Elizabeth.
Dogtag summer / Elizabeth Partridge.
p.   cm.
Summary: In the summer of 1980 before she starts junior high school in Santa Rosa, California,
Tracy, who was adopted from Vietnam when she was six years old, finds an old ammo box with a
dog tag and picture that bring up painful memories for both her Vietnam veteran father and her.
ISBN 978-1-59990-183-1 (hardcover)
[1. Adoption—Fiction. 2. Family life—California—Fiction. 3. Hippies—Fiction. 4. Racially
mixed people—Fiction. 5. Vietnamese Americans—Fiction. 6. Vietnam War, 1961–1975—
Fiction. 7. California—History—1950—Fiction.] I. Title. II. Title: Dog tag summer.
PZ7.P26Do 2011   [Fic]—dc22   2010025515

ISBN 978-1-59990-829-8 (paperback)

Book design by Donna Mark
Typeset by Westchester Book Composition
Printed in the U.S.A. by Quad/Graphics, Fairfield, Pennsylvania
2 4 6 8 10 9 7 5 3 1

All papers used by Bloomsbury Publishing, Inc., are natural, recyclable products
made from wood grown in well-managed forests. The manufacturing processes
conform to the environmental regulations of the country of origin.

Pity them, the souls of those lost thousands.
They must set forth for unknown shores.
They are the ones for whom no incense burns.
Desolate, they wander night after night.

From "Call to Wandering Souls"
Nguyen Du 1765–1820

DOGTAG
SUMMER

Have you ever known absolutely for sure that some piece of you was missing? A piece you buried deep inside and didn't even know was there. Then something cracked open and that missing piece flew out and left an empty, scooped-out place in you, and your heart beat with a longing so strong it sounded like a drum in your ears.

I have. At first I thought it started when Stargazer broke the lock off the old ammo box we found hidden in my garage. Later I realized it began much earlier. Opening the ammo box just let out the ghosts that had been trapped in there for years, waiting.

America, Summer 1980

Stargazer nearly jumped out of his seat when Mrs. McNally asked who would like to take down the bulletin board. He waved his arms back and forth so hard that Mrs. McNally put her hands on her hips and said, "Settle down."

As far as I could tell, nobody else was interested. Jimmie Jones was already hanging out the window banging blackboard erasers together, and most of the class was emptying out their lockers and desks and stuffing things into their backpacks: winter coats, old paperbacks, forks and spoons from the cafeteria.

Stargazer sat back down and put on his best "please, choose me" face. Mrs. McNally relented, no big surprise. Stargazer was one of her favorites.

Instead of walking to the front, Stargazer detoured

down the aisle to my desk. "Had a brain wave," he said, tapping his forehead. "Let's build a Viking funeral ship this summer." Without waiting for an answer, he sprinted up to the bulletin board and started pulling out thumbtacks.

I could see what had given him the idea. After a field trip to San Francisco last fall to see an exhibit about the Vikings, Mrs. McNally had covered the bulletin board with Viking stuff. Right in the middle was a picture from the catalog of the best part of the exhibit: a life-sized replica of a Viking funeral ship. The dead king was lying there in his robes, and around him were all the things he'd need in Viking afterlife: gold jewelry, piles of coins, kettles, swords, and heavy metal war masks.

Around me, people were slamming their desks shut, fake-whispering, throwing things hard into the trash can to make a noise, then acting surprised, like they didn't mean to. It seemed like everybody was looking forward to summer off, looking forward to junior high next fall. Not me. My stomach was in a tight knot. Every time the trash can thunked or somebody dropped a book on the floor, the noise hit me right in the stomach.

Next year we'd be with a bunch of eighth and ninth graders from Santa Rosa. They'd probably ask me stupid questions, like are you an Indian, or Chinese, or what? Or the question I hated the most: do you speak English? Looking at me like they were trying to remember if they'd seen people like me in some *National Geographic* article.

I watched Stargazer pull thumbtacks out of the bulletin board next to the washed-clean blackboard. Suddenly it seemed so empty, like all traces of our class had been washed away. The blackboard didn't belong to us anymore. In a few minutes we were all going to scatter, while Mrs. McNally forgot us and got the blackboard and the room ready for next year.

I opened my empty desk one more time and thought, *it's over.* I glanced up at Mrs. McNally, with her rules and her tidy bun she patted when she was irritated. It was hard to believe, but I was even going to miss Mrs. McNally.

Stargazer wadded up the faded construction paper and threw it out, but made a careful stack of all the Viking pictures. After a brief conference with Mrs. McNally, he took them all back to his desk. He brought a picture of a ship under sail over to me.

"Look," he said. The front prow of the ship cut through foamy white waves, a grimacing dragon's head at the top of a long, arched neck. Intricate carvings of strange-looking animals ran down the neck. Tough-looking men with red beards pulled on the oars, and other men brandished swords and spears and axes.

"Berserkers," he said.

"What?"

"You didn't want to fight with them. They went berserk when they fought, howling and pillaging and plundering."

The thought made my stomach clench even tighter.

"Finish up your jobs, students," said Mrs. McNally. "Five more minutes."

I jumped up. I'd almost forgotten I was supposed to wipe down the class globe, Mrs. McNally's prize possession. I wet a couple of paper towels at the sink and walked over to the bookcase next to the window. Jimmie swung away from the window, and as he walked by me he slapped the erasers together in front of my face.

I ducked, then nearly slugged him. There was barely enough gritty dust left in the erasers to get in my eyes, but for some reason I started to cry, two big fat tears rolling down my cheeks like they were racing each other.

I didn't want to leave Mrs. McNally's class. I didn't want to go to a big new school where I'd have to change classes for each subject, where I might only see Stargazer at lunch. Maybe not even then, since there were two lunch periods.

Jimmie was looking at me like he was surprised and sorry.

"You got chalk in my eyes," I said, and elbowed him hard in the side, which he hated. I knew, because I'd used it before on him when he annoyed me.

"Sorry, sorry," he said, but he was smart enough to walk away and leave me alone.

I wiped my face with the wet paper towels and flipped on the light inside the globe. The oceans glowed light blue near the land, deeper blue out from the shore. I put the tip of my finger where our little town here on the California coast would be if it was big enough to be listed. My fingernail covered the globe from San Francisco up to Point Arena. I slid my finger across the dark, deep waters of the Pacific to the turquoise waters off the coast of Vietnam, then up the green bumpy mountain ridge that curved the length of Vietnam. It felt like the back of a dragon, a little sleeping dragon.

Touching it made me feel . . . not lonely, exactly,

but something way worse. It made me feel *alone*. Like I didn't have anybody to even be lonely for, but was all by myself. Just plain alone. I didn't want to start crying again, so I rubbed my eyes hard with the paper towels.

If anybody asked why my eyes were red, I was going to rat out Jimmie for banging the erasers together in my face. I took in a couple of deep breaths. When I thought I was okay, I steadied the globe with one hand and started wiping it down.

Under the open window a school bus backfired with a bang as it lugged into the waiting zone. The sound ricocheted through me, and suddenly I wasn't here, I was *there*.

Vietnam, Spring 1975

Running on a narrow dirt road next to a river. A sliver of moon hung in the sky, and little fractured moons skittered across the swells of the wide river. The smells of the rice paddies and the river collided on the path as I ran in the dark, thick night.

I heard the growl of a motor up ahead. An American jeep came closer and closer until bright headlights blinded me. I wanted to turn and run the other way, but I didn't. Never run from them, Grandmother had said. You might get shot in the back. So I stood and waited. I sucked in hard breaths, something crumpled tight in my hand, I don't know what. The jeep doors slammed shut and two soldiers ran toward me. My heart made a hammering fear so great hot pee trickled down my leg as I stood to meet my fate in

the bright American headlights. So afraid I didn't even
have words for a prayer to Quan Am. . . .

Right there in room 214 with my finger on the skinny
back of the Vietnam mountain dragon, I knew the
eternal rush and roar and the sound of my heart beating
in my ears was from that moment when pee trickled
down my leg and the moon danced on the river. But
even filled with such a great fear, I knew something for
sure. I belonged *there*, not here.

Suddenly, I slapped the globe—hard—and sent it
spinning around. Mrs. McNally drew in a sharp breath
I heard all the way across the classroom. So did everyone else, because it was suddenly perfectly quiet. She
said, "Tracy," in the cold kind of voice my mother says
would make hell freeze over. "Take your seat."

As I walked back to my desk in that cocoon of
silence, I could still hear the jeep doors slam shut and
heavy American boots thudding in the dirt, coming
straight for me.

~

Stargazer got out of the room first and waited outside
the door for me, the bulletin board papers clutched in

his hand. He started talking a mile a minute, but I couldn't hear a thing. All around us kids whooped and hollered and ran and paid no attention to the teachers yelling "Walk!"

Stargazer grabbed me by the elbow and we shoved our way through the crowded hall. The bus driver had warned us she was keeping to her schedule, last day of school or not. That meant five minutes to get to the bus. No exceptions. Outside, I could finally hear Stargazer.

"It's over!" he was saying. "No more school for three solid months!" He started pushing me toward the bus. He was waving the pictures in the air like they were some kind of award.

"Wait," I said, and pulled my elbow free. "I gotta run to the bathroom."

Stargazer grabbed my arm again and turned with me back toward the bathroom, talking the whole way. I knew he'd stand right outside the door waiting. Any other boy would be mortified, but Stargazer was immune to what other kids thought. It was one of the things I liked best about him, except when it made me mad.

I ducked in and out of the bathroom stall as fast as I could, then stood in front of the row of sinks, running cold water over my hands, listening to all the shouting outside. The bus driver honked her one-minute warning, but inside the bathroom everything stood still.

Stargazer banged on the door and yelled, "Hurry up!"

Water ran through my fingers. The girl staring back at me in the mirror—me—looked shocked, afraid. Out of the slipstream of time, out of place. I was *there*, and now I'm here. What happened?

The door opened a crack and I could see a sliver of Stargazer's face. "What's wrong with you?" he said. "C'mon!"

꒓

We always sat on the driver's side, way back in the second-to-last row, our backpacks on the floor between our calves. I took the window seat in the morning; Stargazer got it in the afternoon. He was still talking a mile a minute. That's part of Stargazer's oblivion: he doesn't care what other people think, but sometimes he doesn't notice what his best friend is thinking either.

I sat next to him, nodding like I was listening, while he flipped through the papers, showing me one after another: ships, chain mail, broadaxes, and helmets. "They'd pillage and get plunder, see?" he kept saying.

Every so often Stargazer ran his hand through his hair, making it stick straight up, a sure sign he was really excited.

Mostly I looked just past him, out the window. Were people taken as plunder? Kids? What had happened when those jeep doors slammed and the huge, shadowy soldiers ran toward me, surrounded by blinding white light?

The bus lurched through a pothole, and Stargazer slammed into my shoulder. I crossed my arms over my stomach, trying to protect myself. Not from Stargazer and the rocking bus, just holding myself tight, so I wouldn't fall any deeper into the scooped-out place opened up by my memories.

"You're not getting carsick, are you?" Stargazer asked. "We haven't even hit the coast yet."

I shook my head, and he flipped to a new page and started in on how the Vikings made sails for the ships.

We pulled out of town and headed up the coast highway, twisting our way along Highway One, the surf smashing into the rocks below, sending up sprays of white water. Just like on Mrs. McNally's globe, the ocean blues got deeper and darker the farther out I looked, till they made a line on the horizon where they met the hazy, pale blue of the sky. How far across the ocean was I seeing? Was the sleeping dragon out there, just past where I could see?

An ocean away from where I belonged . . .

Stargazer was shaking my shoulder. "Your stop's next!" he said. The bus wheels hummed as we hit the bridge crossing the south fork of Switchback River, snaking along the bottom edge of town.

"First stop, Redwood Cove," the bus driver called out, as if we didn't know. I grabbed my backpack, slid forward on the seat. That's another thing the driver didn't put up with: people still collecting their stuff while she was waiting at the stop.

The bus pulled into the dirt parking lot of the Red-wood Cove Market and the doors hissed open. Three younger kids got off before me. "Watch out for cars," the driver warned, like she did at every stop when little kids got off. As I swung off the bus Stargazer yelled at my back, "Ask your parents if you can spend the night tomorrow night! We've got a lot to do!"

The bus rumbled off, dust billowing up around me.

A mother was waiting by a station wagon. I watched as she shepherded the three kids into her car. After they pulled away, I stood in the parking lot, my back to the store. I knew my mother was inside on line two, checking groceries in her brown smock. Up the road about a half a mile, on the edge of town, was Jones Brothers, the lumberyard, where my dad worked. Just beyond was the north fork of Switchback River, where Stargazer got off the bus to walk up the hill to his trailer.

I didn't want to head for my empty, silent house, so I turned and picked my way down the path beside the supermarket. It was steep and narrow, with tough grasses nearly hiding it. Hardly anyone even knew the path was there, it was so overgrown.

Long ago my mother had forbidden me to go down to the ocean here, but there weren't any windows on the side of the supermarket. And in the back—not that my mom could have seen—were floor-to-ceiling cold cases for beer and milk and dairy products, so no one looked out of the store at the ocean.

The path took a steep drop at the corner of the building, so I lowered down on my butt and slid forward, then jumped the last few feet into the pebbly sand. I tumbled onto my knees, and my backpack smacked me on the back of the neck. I stood and brushed off my hands. Warm winds blew down the river as it turned the corner and poured out into the ocean. Although the beach was right out in the open, it was really private, tucked under the cliff and the windowless store. Old redwood stumps and driftwood lay in jumbled piles, thrown way up on the beach by last winter's storms. Shorebirds ran back and forth at the water's edge, calling each other with their sad, piercing cry: "*Too-et, too-et.*"

I kicked off my shoes, then crossed the sand and waded out knee-deep in the waves, felt them swirl and froth around my knees. The plaintive sound of the shorebirds was drowned out by the roar of the waves as they came in, and the clatter and slither of pebbles as the waves dragged them back into the ocean. Every time a wave sucked back out it pulled sand and pebbles from under my feet too.

I stared way out across the ocean. Where had I been running so fast when the bright lights of the jeep caught me? What was I running from?

Far out past the breakers a huge wave gathered, swelled, then rolled toward the beach. It came faster, gathering speed, gray-blue and fringed with dirty white foam, hungry to drag me out to sea and pull me along the ocean floor with the sand and pebbles.

I turned and ran up the beach, out of reach of the treacherous wave, wishing I could have run from the jeep long, long ago.

ꝏ

Dad pushed the green beans on his plate into a pile, then stabbed four or five with his fork, swiped them through his mashed potatoes, and shoved them into his mouth. Mom winced but didn't say anything. Instead she turned to look at me.

"So how was the last day of school?" she asked.

I shrugged. "Pretty much the same."

"Did you do anything special?"

Yeah, I thought, *I slapped the world and set it spinning.* Actually, I realized I used to belong next to a river, a different river, tucked under the blue-green belly of the dragon mountains.

Mom stared at me, her eyes tired and sad looking. She pushed a few strands of hair behind her ear.

"Tracy?" she said. She was still wearing her brown smock from work, a sure sign she'd had a long, exhausting day, because she usually stripped it off as soon as she finished her shift. "You must have done *something* different."

I thought for a second. "We cleaned out our desks. And at lunch the cafeteria ladies gave each of us a huge cupcake, which they said was to thank us for being sweet kids. They even gave one to Jimmie, who started a food fight a few months ago, but first they made him promise he wouldn't do it again." I didn't mention he smeared all his frosting off on the underside of the table.

"Oh, and Mrs. McNally wrote 'Have a Happy, Safe Summer' on the blackboard." Before even that got washed away.

The mention of a safe summer set Mom off. "Are you sure you don't want to go to the Y day camp?" she asked. "I bet they still have room—"

"Mom," I interrupted, "you already said I don't have to go." But for just a second, I wondered if I should change my mind and give in. Get up in the morning, take the little jitney with the whale painted on the side to Ukiah. But then I remembered how we did the same art projects year after year and played girls' softball every afternoon. I was way better than all the other girls, but they'd never let our team play the boys because they said we might get hurt.

Instead, I could go over to Stargazer's, where his parents pretty much let us do whatever we wanted. Besides, I'd stayed by myself on Saturdays for the last year when my mom pulled weekend shift.

Mom was looking at me like she might start going over the whole thing again.

"I've got other plans for the summer," I blurted out.

"She'll be fine, Donna," said my dad. "When we were kids we were on our own all summer long. We'd just show up for dinner, muddy and tired." He took a swallow from the tall glass of bourbon and water he drank every night.

"I know, I know," said my mom. "But times have changed." She started in on her litany of worries, things that might hurt me: strangers, the ocean, cars, germs, rabid dogs.

The rush and roar and fear from the classroom filled my ears again, drowning out her words. Bright lights of the American jeep and thudding footsteps seemed to come straight for me again.

I grabbed tight to my fork, felt the metal press into my skin. *What was happening to me?* I stared at Mom as she cut a tidy bite of meat off her hamburger. *How about American GIs?* I thought. *They should be on the top of your list of dangers.*

I shot a quick glance at Dad, spearing green beans. He was hunched over his plate, one elbow on the table. In the living room is a photo of my parents getting married in someone's backyard. My mom's wearing a simple sleeveless dress. He's in uniform, standing up tall, looking at the camera, grinning.

An army uniform. How many times had I walked right past that photo without really looking at it? Hundreds of times? Thousands?

I pushed my chair back and stood up. "May I please be excused?"

Mom sighed, waved a hand in the air. "Just go," she said. "Put your plate in the dishwasher."

I scraped the last of the mashed potatoes off my plate and dropped it in the dishwasher along with my glass.

On my way to my room I stopped in front of Mom and Dad's wedding photo. Here's what I knew about my dad and the armed services: He served in the army in Vietnam. He and my mom married just before he was sent over. He came back (said my mom, one time): "different."

We never, ever talked about it.

~

In the morning, I heard the back door close and Dad's feet crunch on the gravel driveway. He made a few trips between the garage and his truck, loading stuff into the big white toolbox in the truck bed. He slammed the toolbox shut then rapped on the window right next to my bed. "Bye, chickadee," he said.

He'd done that every morning since I could remember, Monday through Friday at 7:20, 8:20 on Saturday. He said the only good thing about working Saturdays was that he didn't have to be at work until 8:30 instead of 7:30. Other than that, he hated Saturdays because the store was full of people working on their home projects. Orders were small, and every do-it-yourself guy hung around, asking for free advice. The carpenters who came in during the week just put in their material orders, loaded up, and left.

The warm smell of coffee wafted in from the kitchen,

and I heard the newspaper rustle as Mom turned the page. I rolled over and nestled back into my covers.

I liked Saturday mornings. Sleeping in. Even my dad's light footsteps on the gravel seemed slower, more relaxed. But this morning something was tugging at me, a vague worry swimming around in the back of my mind.

Swam closer. Smacking the globe. *There.*

Then a thought hit me so fast I sat straight up in bed: the photo album. Where did Mom keep it? My mother carefully put in photos of me every year: first day of school, school plays, birthday cakes, and Christmas stockings. I swung my feet out of bed. Maybe there'd be something in there, a hint, a clue. I didn't usually like to look at the photos in the album. Mom always made me stare straight at the camera and smile, like I was completing a perfect picture she had already set up in her mind.

"You're up early," Mom said when I padded into the kitchen in my bathrobe.

"Uh-huh," I said. I sat down, looked at her hands holding the newspaper in front of her as she read. For a second I thought of asking her where the photo album was, then decided not to. I wanted to find it on my own, look at the pictures by myself.

I poured myself a bowl of Cheerios, then asked, "What're you doing today?"

"The usual," she answered, without putting down the paper. "Bank. Groceries." Mom never shopped on the same days she worked. She said she liked to walk in without her smock on and be treated like a regular customer.

"And Becky's going to cut my hair," she added. Mom traded haircuts with another checker at the supermarket, who had curly hair like hers. Sometimes they did manicures for each other too. Mom said it was almost as good as driving down to Santa Rosa and getting pampered at a real salon.

I smashed a mouthful of Cheerios on the roof of my mouth, swallowed. "Can I spend the night at Stargazer's tonight?"

Mom put down the newspaper and looked at me. She was wearing a pale blue tank top. For work they had to wear sleeves, and she loved having her arms bare. "May I," she said.

"May I?" I asked. Mom was worse than Mrs. McNally for proper grammar.

"Tracy, you aren't planning to spend all summer with him, are you?"

"No," I said. "It's just . . . he asked me to help him with a project. A big one this time. He wants to build a Viking ship." I left off the word *funeral,* in case it would somehow make her worry. "It's very educational," I added.

Her face softened. "It is the first day of summer, isn't it. Okay, but come home after breakfast tomorrow." She drained her coffee cup and stood up. "I used to love lazy summer days. I didn't get too many of them—my mother had me running to ballet and music and French lessons most of the time."

Mom folded the paper and put her dishes in the sink. "But just because school's out doesn't mean chores stop, you know."

ॐ

It was after eleven before Mom finally left. By then she'd vacuumed the whole house. She started up front in her bedroom, like she always did, and worked her way back through the bathroom, living room, kitchen, and my room. While she vacuumed and cleaned the bathroom, I folded and put away two loads of laundry, cleared the dishwasher, emptied all the wastebaskets, and took out the kitchen garbage. By now, it was a tradition: me and Mom, cleaning the house together.

I had spotted the pink photo album on the highest shelf of the living room bookcase while I was emptying the wastebaskets. As soon as Mom drove away I pulled it down and sat on the couch with it on my lap. I ran my fingers over the words on the front of the slippery plastic cover. "Our Daughter," it said in curlicue script.

I opened it. A photo was glued right in the middle of the first page.

The picture was me, standing by my bed. I still had the same bedspread, but now it was faded to a pale yellow. I was wearing a striped T-shirt and a pair of green pants with white stitching around the pockets. My sleeves and pant legs were rolled up, and a belt held the pants bunched around my waist.

Underneath was the date, April 10, 1975, in my mother's careful handwriting. "Tracy comes home."

Home, I thought. Home. The word made a soft humming sound in my ears. Had I run away from my Vietnamese home-by-the-river?

Vietnam, Autumn 1974

I stood on the porch, staring up the dirt path that ran in front of our hut.

Waiting so long made my chest ache.

Má hadn't come to see us since the rice was young in the fields. She'd left, murmuring promises that she'd be back soon, but the rice had ripened in the long, hot days of summer, and still we hadn't seen her. Would she come today for mid-autumn festival, bringing me a lantern shaped like a moon or a hare?

I left the shady porch and stood in the middle of the path, our hut on one side, the wide brown river sliding by on the other. Far in the distance two boys were walking away, heading toward the big paved road where trucks and motorcycles and bicycles thrummed back and forth. Was Má on the road right now, pedaling her way here?

Grandmother brushed past me, carrying a heavy basket of fish across the path to the river. She squatted in the shallow water, the basket on the bank beside her. I went back to the shaded porch and watched her slit open each fish with the tip of her knife, swish it through the tea-colored water, then throw the cleaned fish back in the basket.

The lapping current of the river carried the fish guts slowly downstream. Just past Grandmother's canoe, small silvery fish flashed out from under the monkey bridge to the outhouse built over the river. They grabbed the fish guts and disappeared back in the shadows.

"She will come if she can," Grandmother called over her shoulder, feeling my waiting. She threw the last cleaned fish in the basket, and stood up, rubbing her back.

Just when I was about to give up and go inside, I saw a bike way down the path, coming our way, fast. When it got closer I saw it was Má, her lavender ao dai flapping around her legs. Behind her, a star-shaped lantern bobbed on a thin bamboo pole.

I wanted to rush out to greet her when she pulled to a stop, see what was in the box strapped to the back of the bike. But longing and shyness crowded together in my chest. My feet moved slowly to the path.

"*I brought you a lantern for the festival tonight,*" *she said, her smile filling her whole face.* "*And moon cakes full of sweet lotus-seed paste.*"

I touched her hand, only one word in my mouth. "*Má,*" *I said.*

She pulled me close. Her black hair fell around me; it smelled of American shampoo. "*Someday,*" *she whispered,* "*when the war is over, I will take you to live with me in Da Nang.*"

Someday was a long, long time away.

I flipped through the pink album. It was just as I remembered: the first day of every school year, birthday cakes, my new bike, Easter egg hunts in the park. I turned back to the first page. Bangs were cut ragged across my forehead, and I was clutching a stiff plastic doll with yellow hair. I looked absolutely terrified.

I didn't even hear my mom come in the living room, but suddenly she was there, standing over me.

"Forgot my shopping list," she said. She looked down at my lap. "You looking at your baby book?" she said. Anger surged through me. Why did she always call this my baby book? I was never a baby *here*, I was a baby *there*. The couch dipped as she sat down next to me. "Look how small you were. When we heard you were at the airport, we stopped at Sears on the way down and bought clothes the saleslady said were for six-year-olds." She smiled. "We probably should have bought clothes for a four-year-old, you were so tiny and skinny."

I knew the story: we wanted a little girl, and you needed a family. But if they had wanted me so much, why weren't they ready? I looked carefully for the right words. I didn't want to sound as angry as I felt. "You only stopped then? Didn't you know ahead of time I was coming?"

"Sweetie, there was a war going on; the communication was terrible. You came over in a planeload of orphans. It was complete chaos."

"What was?"

She shook her head at the memory. "The airport. There were so many of you, and these exhausted women who'd been on the flight, trying to take care of all of you. There was even a class of first-year medical students from Davis checking you over. Sick, crying kids, all these med students in white lab coats looking freaked out. What a mess."

"Did you know which one was me?"

"No. We were trying to guess, but we were looking for a bigger girl."

I tapped the photo. "Was this my very first day?" I was reaching, looking for a clue that would bridge the gap between *there* and *here*.

"No, that's the second or third day." Mom leaned over my shoulder to look more closely. "I didn't take a picture of you the first day. You were so filthy when you arrived. I finally got your clothes off while you were sleeping. When you woke up—we'd put this nightie on you that was huge—you kept patting your chest and saying something in Vietnamese."

"What was I saying?"

Mom shrugged. "Probably something like 'Where's my shirt?' You started running all over the house, crying, pulling open drawers, looking in the kitchen cupboards. Dad tried to pick you up, but you bit him."

I *bit* my dad? I felt a tunnel of emptiness and shame open up in me. "I did? Where?"

"On the hand. Then you ran for the back door."

"What did he do?"

"He reached for you again—we were both scared what would happen if you got outside. Where would you run to?"

"Did I bite him again?"

"No, you dodged past him and ran to your room and hid in the closet. You hid in your closet a lot in those first months, whenever you got upset. Dad used to sit on the floor outside your closet and sing songs to you."

"What songs?" *Maybe it's just little tiny pieces,* I thought. Little pieces that will make a bridge back to *there.*

"You're sure full of questions this morning," she said. "Um . . ." She leaned back and hummed to herself for a moment. "Simon and Garfunkel, Aretha Franklin, Marvin Gaye."

"Who are they?"

"Oh, folk and soul singers. I'm trying to remember . . . your dad had this one Beatles song he used to sing to you all the time . . . 'Hey Jude.'"

She stood up. "It all seems like so long ago," she said. "Don't forget to lock up when you leave, and make sure you have your key."

"I've got it, Mom." I tapped my chest. I always wore my key on a long chain, hanging down inside my shirt. I never had to take it off—I could just pull it out of my shirt, and bend forward to unlock the door.

Mom leaned over and kissed me on the cheek. "I'd forgotten how rough it was when you first got here," she said. "Those first few months, I thought we were going to spend our lives trying to coax you out of hiding."

I sat still on the couch after the door shut behind her. Thoughts tumbled around in my head, fell down into the hollow, scooped-out space inside me.

I'd had a home by a wide, tea-colored river. I'd had Grandmother and Má. Before my baby book started when I was six, before I used to hide in my closet, I'd been a baby to somebody else.

༃

I gave a couple of last hard pushes on the pedals of my bike and pulled up in the field in front of Stargazer's mobile home. My hands were burning from hanging on to the jumpy handlebars as I pedaled up the twisty road to his property. Strapped onto the back of the bike I had a bundle with my pajamas, toothbrush, and hairbrush. At the last minute I threw my bathing suit in.

Stargazer's dogs, Jip and Pixie, burst out from under the mobile home, a blur of black and white, barking like crazy. When they were a few feet away they recognized me and started yipping a welcome. Pixie crouched low, her wagging tail throwing up plumes of dust as if she were apologizing for not knowing it was me sooner. Jip threw himself at me, his front paws up on my chest, nearly knocking me over. I put my arm up to try to keep Jip from licking my face, but really I loved it. Jip was so wholehearted. I wanted him to lick away all the confused, empty feelings inside me.

The door opened and Stargazer's mother, Ruthie, came out with his little sister, Summer, on her hip. Summer's legs gripped tightly around one of Ruthie's legs below her round, pregnant belly.

"Oh hi, Tracy," Ruthie said. Her face broke into a smile. Between her and the dogs, I felt something inside me relax. "Jip, down," Ruthie said, but she didn't really mean it. Summer leaned against her mother's shoulder, her blond hair snarled, two bright red patches on her cheeks. "Come on in," Ruthie said. "I'm just making some herbal tea for Summer. She's sick. Stargazer's around here somewhere."

I wheeled my bike over to the side of the house and leaned it against the woodpile. Pixie slipped up beside me and butted her nose in my hand, asking for attention. I gave her a good rub around the ears. I liked the feeling of her broad head between my hands. Then I climbed up the rickety stairs into the trailer. Hot, steamy air hit me as I walked in. A big pot boiled on the stove, filling the air with the tangy smell of fresh herbs. Little drops of water ran down the steamed-up windows.

"I've got some peppermint and yarrow leaves in here," Ruthie said. She readjusted Summer on her hip and stirred the pot. "I'm trying to get her fever down."

Ruthie looked beautiful with her hair in messy curls and the room all steamy and blurry behind her. I stood beside her and watched her stir. I liked how Ruthie never fussed over me or asked me the kind of stupid questions adults came up with. She just seemed to fold me into the rest of the family.

Ruthie rubbed her lower back and tried to slide Summer down to the floor, but Summer whimpered and wriggled back up in her arms. "Oh, Summer," Ruthie groaned.

"Here, hold her, Tracy, while I strain the tea." She unpeeled Summer and pushed her into my arms. Summer howled and lurched back toward her mother, throwing me off balance for a second.

"Take her outside, okay?" Ruthie said over Summer's roaring.

I headed out. Another thing I loved about being at Stargazer's was that something was always happening, unlike at my quiet house. "Come on, Summer," I said. "Let's go find Jip and Pixie."

They found us the second I sat down with Summer on the top step of the porch. They ran up the stairs, tipped their heads sideways, and both tried to lick Summer's face at the same time, whining with concern. Summer wove her fingers into Jip's ruff and buried her face in his fur.

Stargazer appeared around the corner of the trailer, holding his notebook. He didn't see me until he got to the bottom of the stairs and looked up. Summer pulled out of my arms and flung herself at him.

"Whoa," he said, staggering backward under her weight. He tossed his notebook on the stair beside me and sat down on it. Summer leaned into his chest and stuck her thumb in her mouth. In the sudden quiet her thumb-sucking made a slurpy wet sound.

A sharp pang of jealousy hit me right in the chest. I felt bad being jealous of Summer, but I was. She was so trusting. She had so many people she could melt against. And then I was jealous of Stargazer, that she wanted to melt onto him more than me.

"You ought to try sharing a bed with her sometime," said Stargazer. Just when I thought Stargazer was oblivious, he'd respond to something I didn't even quite know I was feeling.

"My parents said she has to start sleeping with me," he went on, "because they need room in their bed for the new baby. They want Summer to get used to my bed before the baby comes."

Stargazer's parents slept in a double bed at one end of the trailer, and the built-in dinette table at the other end dropped down even with the bench seats and made a bed for Stargazer. It made me wonder: how would the new baby fit in the trailer, into their lives? It was already so crowded.

"How can you both fit in that little bed?" I asked. "We sleep head to toe," Stargazer said, "like two sardines in a tin can. And she kicks."

Summer pulled her thumb out of her mouth. "Do not," she said, and stuck her thumb back in.

"How would you know?" said Stargazer. "You're asleep."

Summer swung her leg back and kicked him right in the calf.

"Ow!" he said, but I could tell he wasn't mad.

"I was looking for stuff to make the Viking ship," he said to me, "but I couldn't find much."

"What do we need?" I asked.

"I'll show you," he said. He grabbed his notebook and opened it up to a big, two-page drawing he'd made of the ship. "We'll need some wood to make the ship, and cloth for the sails." He tapped the dragon's head he'd drawn at the front. "I haven't figured out yet how we're going to make the dragon."

He'd drawn the head like a dog's skull, with small ears pricked forward. The mouth was frightening. It looked like a sea serpent's, with a long tongue circling out between sharp, bared teeth.

"Carve it?" I suggested.

"Maybe," he said. "Does your dad have any chisels?"

"I don't know," I said. I wasn't sure what tools my dad had. And suddenly the whole idea of making something so scary worried me.

"Let's go look in your dad's garage, see what he's got that we could use."

"How about tomorrow," I said. I didn't want to leave his house after I just got here. Besides, I felt safe here, free of the scooped-out feeling and those strange memories that were suddenly taking hold of me. "I brought my bathing suit," I added.

Stargazer grinned at me. "Yeah," he said. "Let's go for a swim. We can start the ship tomorrow."

He tossed his notebook back on the porch.

࿓

I thought I was going to leave it alone, but I couldn't.

"I've got a question for you," I said to Stargazer. He was lying next to me on the hot rocks by the river. We'd walked past the vegetable garden and out to the river. We'd gone upstream, hiking along the sandy edge until the river swung in a lazy arc and the water made a deep, slow-moving pool.

For a long time we'd tried to catch a crayfish in the pool, avoiding the fast-moving whirlpool near the far bank. We'd stayed in the water until we were so cold we could barely move. Our wet bathing suits practically sizzled on the flat, hot rocks that lined one bank of the river. I looked at my arms: goose pimples made all the hairs stand straight up.

Stargazer poked me.

"You going to ask me your question or not?" he said.

I rolled over onto my back on a dry patch of rock. The backs of my legs stung with the heat and I almost rolled back to the spot that had already cooled off.

"Yeah," I answered. "What's your first memory of me?"

"Hmm," he said. "I didn't really pay much attention to you at first."

"Think," I said. I reached over and tapped his forehead the way he did when he had a brain wave.

"Well, you were different looking. Skinny and serious. You never smiled. You weren't like the other girls, that's for sure."

"When did we start being friends?"

"I remember *that*," said Stargazer. "There was a circle of boys on the playground one day. Something about the way they were bunched together . . . I went over to see why. They had you surrounded. You had your fists up, like you were going to fight them all."

My breath caught. I remembered. I'd been here for a few months, maybe for a year? I'd stolen somebody's lunch at recess and eaten the baloney sandwich and the Hostess Twinkies. The boys caught me with the empty bag in my hand, and were tightening around me, moving in. "Gook, gook," they had chanted. "Go home, gook."

Vietnam, Autumn 1974

Grandmother gave me an empty can and sent me out to gather snails for soup. I ran across the path and splashed into the river water. I didn't want to miss a moment with Má. I didn't want to miss a word, or a touch. The long-legged birds picking their way between the weeds flew up, wings beating, with their lonely cry: too-et, too-et. I floated the can in the water next to me, ran my hands up and down the water-covered stems, feeling for snails, dropping them into the can.

A schoolboy I didn't know rode toward me on his bike. "Con lai," he yelled as he came close. Half-breed.

I hated the boys in their fancy school uniforms. Má and Grandmother would never have enough money for books and school fees. Grandmother said it was hard enough just to keep food in my belly.

"Half-breed," the boy yelled again as he pedaled by. "Go live with your rich father in America!"

I grabbed a big snail from my can and threw it as hard as I could at his back, hoping it would smash into his white shirt, make a trail of muddy water down his back.

But I missed and the boy was gone, leaving con lai ringing in my ears.

I remembered those boys chanting "gook." Right there on the playground I had dropped the lunch bag and spun around, looking for the weakest one, so I could knock him to the ground and run. I remembered how Stargazer had suddenly appeared in the circle, pulling two boys apart by the shoulders.

"Leave her alone," he'd said. "Why're you picking on a girl?" Serious eyes the color of the ocean. The boys had fallen back, glanced around, and melted away.

Now Stargazer flipped over carefully on the hot river rocks. "You looked like you meant business," he said. "After that I tried to teach you the names of all the presidents. I figured you needed to prove to people you were as American as them, in case they called you names again. You could have just recited the whole list of presidents, fast—rat-a-tat-a-tat."

Typical Stargazer solution. Overwhelm them with information.

He heaved up on his elbow and stared at me. "But you never memorized them, did you?"

"No." I shook my head. "But I never stole anyone's lunch again."

"Poor Coolidge," he said, and lay back down on the rocks.

"Who?"

"Calvin Coolidge. Hardly anyone even knows he was president."

"Stargazer?"

"What?"

"Just shut up, okay?" I said.

✧

After dinner Ruthie sent us outside to set up our sleeping bags. Stargazer and I spread a tarp out on the grass behind the trailer and laid our bags on top. Ruthie seemed surprised when Stargazer told her I was spending the night and asked me if it was okay with my parents. "Of course," Stargazer had answered before I could say anything. "Well, we're not their favorite people in the world," Ruthie had answered mildly.

When we walked back around to the front, Ruthie was sitting on the top stair and Summer was on the stair below, leaning on Ruthie's legs. Stargazer and I sat down on either side of Ruthie. Through the open door we could hear Stargazer's father, Beldon, washing the dishes. The sky was deepening into purple, and a thin crescent moon was already high in the sky.

Out behind the garden the river murmured, like someone humming a song. I was full from brown rice with turnip greens that Beldon had picked in the garden and big, soft squares of tofu. All flavored with soy sauce and fresh ginger.

Ruthie leaned against me and whispered, "Feel this, Tracy." She took my hand, laid it on her round belly, and flattened her hand over mine. "Shhh," she said, even though I hadn't said anything. "Just wait. You'll feel the baby kick."

Then suddenly I did. There was a bump under my palm, then another and another. Ruthie smiled. "That's the baby's feet. She's dancing."

And she was. I could feel her feet bumping and sliding, as if she was listening to music we couldn't hear.

"Maybe she's doing a dance to the moon," I whispered.

"That's it!" said Ruthie. "Let's call her Moon Dance."

"Ruthie," groaned Stargazer. "Can't you just name the baby something normal?"

I was surprised. Kids sometimes teased Stargazer about his name, but I didn't know it bothered him.

"Like what?" Ruthie didn't seem upset. "Her name matches yours. Like two bookends around Summer."

"How about if you just go with the S theme. Stargazer, Summer, um . . . Sam! If it's a girl, her name could be Samantha."

"Nope," said Ruthie. "There was a girl in my junior high school named Samantha. She was a holy terror. Tons of black eyeliner, bleached blond hair. She used to shake us down for our lunch money in the bathroom. Which she gave to her high school boyfriend to buy cigarettes for her."

I liked how Stargazer's parents talked to him like he was a friend. My parents were much more careful about what they said to me. I'd even been in the trailer one time when Ruthie and Beldon had fought, yelling at each other about money. My parents never argued in front of me.

"Okay, okay," Stargazer said. "How about something really ordinary, like Sara or Amber or something."

Just then Beldon yelled from inside the trailer. "Look what I found!" He came to the door with a colander and held it down for us to see. "The strawberries we were *supposed* to have for dessert," he said. There was a big bite taken out of each one.

Summer hid her face against Ruthie's leg.

"You've got to keep a better eye on her," Beldon said irritably to Ruthie.

"She's sick, honey," Ruthie said. "Come on, time for bed everybody."

"I picked them for all of us, not just her," Beldon said.

Ruthie didn't answer, just took Summer into the bathroom while Stargazer and I stood at the kitchen counter and ate the strawberries. Beldon said he didn't want any, and got the bedding out to make up the bed for Summer.

I leaned my elbows on the counter while Stargazer looked through the *North Coast Observer*. He flipped through a couple of pages, then ran his finger down the tiny writing on the "Sun and Moon and Ocean Tides" column.

"Here it is," he said, nudging me with his elbow. "The moon sets at ten thirty tonight. If we stay awake, we'll get some good stargazing in." He grinned at me. I guess he didn't feel that bad about his name.

"Make sure your faces are clean," said Beldon. He laughed and snapped the dish towel at Stargazer. "You don't want some raccoon licking you in the middle of night, trying to get that strawberry juice off your face."

He swept the little pile of strawberry tops off the counter and dumped them into the compost bucket.

"Beldon," said Ruthie, coming out of the bathroom with Summer, both of them smelling like mint tooth-paste. "Don't scare them. Who's next for the bathroom?"

✵

I lay on my back in the sleeping bag. The sun was long gone, but a red smudge still lay on the horizon, outlining the hills. The moon was tipped on its back like a bowl, and the stars were soft silver specks in the sky. Beside me, I could hear Stargazer breathing deep and slow.

I must have fallen asleep, because the next time I looked for the moon it had gone down. The stars were bright, like someone had turned up the voltage. There were millions and millions and millions of them.

A tiny silver streak shot across the sky.

I nudged Stargazer and he woke up with a start. "What?" he said.

"Time to look for shooting stars."

We both saw the next two that fired off, one right after the other.

"Wow," said Stargazer. I heard the rustle of his notebook.

"What are you doing?"

"Making a mark every time I see a shooting star."

"Why?"

"For luck."

"Luck for what?"

"Nothing. Just luck."

"Why? Do you think you can you gather luck and save it?" I asked him.

"That's a metaphysical question," he said. "I'm better at science."

We were quiet for a minute, just waiting for another shooting star, then Stargazer said, "Do you ever think about all those stars out there? Like how big the whole universe is and how tiny we are?"

Stargazer kept talking, his voice swirling around me like a misty rain, his words soft and excited as he talked about the speed of light and how far away the stars were and the big bang theory.

"It's all expanding, even right now," he said. "Can you feel it, how the stars are all getting farther and farther away every second?"

I stared up into the shimmering stars, following Stargazer's excitement, trying to open myself up to the enormity of all those pinpricks of light. Suddenly they tipped and swam and I was running along that dirt path in Vietnam in my bare feet, the smell of rice paddies and river and gas fumes in my nose. I felt so afraid I gasped out loud.

"I know," said Stargazer. "When you really think about it, it's so cool."

꒜

After a late breakfast at Stargazer's I rode my bike home. Dad was already settled on the couch watching a baseball game on TV and Mom had started one of her Sunday baking projects. When I walked into the kitchen, flour and sugar canisters were out on the counter and she was grabbing something out of an overhead cabinet.

"Did you have a good time at Stargazer's?" she asked as she pulled down a yellow box of cornstarch.

"Um-hum," I answered. While she measured out flour and salt, I told her about sitting on the porch watching the moon, and that Stargazer had drawn plans for the Viking ship, but there was a lot I skipped. Sleeping outside would have been bad enough, but swimming in the river by ourselves probably would have gotten me grounded for life.

"Grab the eggs from the fridge, okay, sweetie?" she said. "You can separate six of them for me. Oh, and I need a stick of butter for the crust."

I pulled the eggs and butter out and set them on the kitchen table. Usually I loved baking with Mom: beating the eggs, adding in sugar and flour, licking the empty bowl. Mom's specialty was cakes: rich German chocolate with coconut and pecans in the frosting; tall, spongy angel food cake with icing drizzled on. Any time the PTA held a bake sale, other mothers bid high for her cakes.

I slid the butter out of the carton and handed it to Mom. "A crust?" I said. She wasn't usually big on making pies.

Mom peeled the wrapper off the butter. "Today

we're making lemon meringue pie. Lemon custard for the sun, meringue for the clouds. Like a summer sky. We used to have them on . . ." She stopped, cut the stick of butter into the flour. "I think the Fourth of July. After we went to the big parade—and growing up in Washington DC, I mean *big*—floats, marching bands, speeches, the works." She glanced up at the clock. "I'll ask my mother when she calls. I haven't been to a parade since I was a kid. Your dad hates Fourth of July parades. Too many firecrackers. Too much noise. Too many people."

Mom smashed the butter into the flour with a fork, sending up small floury geysers. For a minute I felt like I was standing back and watching her, instead of really working with her. Cakes and pies seemed so American all of a sudden. Apple pie. Fourth of July. Lemon meringue pie. My mind raced as I separated the eggs, passing the egg yolk back and forth between the two half shells, letting the egg whites slide into a stainless steel bowl under my hands.

Did I even eat eggs in Vietnam? "What did I like to eat when I first came here?" I asked.

"At first, only Jell-O and plain noodles. I remember one time when we'd had you just a couple of days, and I came in the kitchen, and you'd found a can of evaporated milk and somehow opened it with a knife. I couldn't believe you didn't cut yourself. You were hiding under the table, drinking it straight from the can."

Another thing I didn't remember.

I was just putting the egg carton back in the fridge when Mom reached over to get an ice cube from the freezer and we bumped lightly into each other. She wrapped her arms around me and gave me a hug.

"Look how tall you've gotten," she said, but she didn't let me go. I was surprised to feel how tall I was: the top of my head came up to her shoulder. I could feel my breasts, like little quail eggs, pressing into my mom's softness. I was too surprised to even be embarrassed.

Mom must have felt the same thing, because she pulled back and gave my shoulders a quick squeeze. "You're growing up," she said, like it was the first time she realized it. "My little girl." Her eyes were soft and proud as she searched my face, like I'd done something amazing.

"Mom," I protested. Now I was embarrassed. I could feel my face flush red and I looked away.

The phone rang, and Mom jumped. She glanced at the kitchen clock. "My mother," she said. "Right on time." She reached for the princess phone hanging on the wall.

"Hello, Mother," she said. "Yes, I knew it was you." She slipped her hand over the receiver and giggled at me. "I guess I'm psychic or something. Yes, Mother, I'm listening," she said into the phone. I could hear a tinny stream of words coming from the phone. Mom rolled her eyes at me, and hunched her shoulder up to cradle the phone so she could keep pressing the back of the fork into the flour and butter.

She turned back toward me and covered the receiver again. "Go grab five or six lemons off the tree, okay?"

I was glad to escape to the backyard. My grandmother called every Sunday to talk to my mother, but I'd only met her once, three years ago at her fancy apartment in Washington DC.

"So this is the little girl," my grandmother had said, tipping my face up by my chin. She had gray hair piled in high stiff curls and rings sparkling on her fingers.

"Our daughter," Mom had said, an edge in her voice. I'd already been in America for two years. My grandmother had let go of my chin and looked at my mother, twisting her wedding ring on her finger.

"Of course. Your daughter," she said. "Do stop twisting your ring, dear. It's very unbecoming."

Mom had flushed, and dropped her hands to her sides.

"You may call me Grandee," she said to me.

But I didn't. I avoided calling her anything for the next two days while we went to the Smithsonian and walked through art museums and sat in restaurants where Mom ordered fruit salad for me, because my stomach was in a tight knot. By the end of the visit my mother looked like she was about to shatter like a piece of glass hit just right by a little stone. I didn't feel much better.

Vietnam, Autumn 1974

When the full moon rose and a pathway of moonlight shimmered on the water, Grandmother lit the candle in my lantern and the three of us walked beside the river into the village, my star following behind me. On every path were the shadowy shapes of the villagers, lanterns flickering with candles: tigers, carps, frogs, and butterflies danced behind them. I was swept along in the lights.

In the soft light of the lanterns none of the schoolboys could see I was con lai, half-blood. Just for tonight no one could see the stamp of my American father in my brown hair and round eyes.

Finally the candle in my lantern burned out and we walked home, my stomach full of fruit and moon cakes. On the front porch Má knelt next to me, her cheek against mine. She pointed at the moon, now high and far away in *the sky, and whispered to me. Her words came fast and urgent, dropping on top of each other.* "Never forget," *she whispered to me.* "Never forget."

I tugged a couple of lemons off the tree next to the garage. Luckily, I didn't have to talk to my grandmother very often. Mom kept her updated on what I was doing. She had a fake cheerful way of talking to Grandee, keeping her away while pretending she was holding her close.

I was just piling the lemons in the crook of my arm to reach for one more when Stargazer skidded around the corner on his bike. He jumped off and leaned it against the garage.

"Ready to look for supplies?" he said.

"Sure," I said. I knew Mom would have to chill the pie crust for a while before she'd need the lemons for the custard. I dropped the lemons onto the ground under the tree.

I had to shove against the door to the garage with my shoulder to get it open. When it suddenly gave, I nearly fell onto the floor. "Wow," said Stargazer over my shoulder. "This place is gloomy." From the back wall, a little light came in through a filthy, vine-covered window.

Stargazer went into curious mode, walking around in front of the shelves, staring at everything, touching things: old gallons of paint, aerosol cans, boxes of screws and nails, garden tools. We were right in the middle of Dad's territory in here. Even Mom had given up trying to make him keep it clean.

Stargazer walked around the lawn mower and kicked through a pile of old sawdust on the floor between Dad's table saw and drill press.

"What kind of supplies are you looking for?" I asked him.

"Don't know yet," he said. He pulled a piece of plywood from where it was leaning against the wall, then dropped it back. "This would be impossible to work with."

"We could get my dad to help us," I said.

Stargazer shook his head. "No way. It's summer vacation. That means no adults telling us what to do."

I was glad. I really didn't want to stand around and watch my dad and Stargazer do a project together while I got stuck making iced tea and sandwiches for them.

"Hey, what's this?" Stargazer said, and tugged on a piece of old sheet metal that was propped against one of the shelves. He untucked his shirt and his notebook fell out. He opened it to his picture of the ship and squinted at it. "We could cut out circles of this sheet metal to make the shields that go along the sides."

"We'd need some of my dad's big scissors that cut metal."

"They're called sheet metal shears," he said.

"Fine," I snapped. Sometimes I got tired of Stargazer knowing everything. "The hard part is going to be finding them."

I was on one side of the garage looking through piles of things like hammers and screwdrivers when Stargazer gave a low whistle. There was a screech of metal sliding on the cement floor.

"Maybe there are sheet metal tools in here," Stargazer said.

He hoisted up a metal box about the size of my backpack, but skinnier. It looked like it could hold tools. He shook it, and something made a thunking noise inside. "Too lightweight for tools," he said. He put it back on the floor. "Wait a sec," he said, and dropped to his knees.

He spit on top of the box and rubbed it with his shirtsleeve.

"I think it's an ammo box," he said, and spit again. "Something's written on top." He started running his hand through his hair.

"Ammo?" I asked, leaning over him.

"Ammunition box."

I wanted two things in one blinding moment: I wanted him to put it back, fast, while I ran out of the garage. And I wanted to grab the box away from him, touch it, open it, see what was inside.

I was standing completely still, thoughts colliding in my head, when Stargazer walked out of the garage with the box.

By the time I got outside he was squatting down in front of it. I dropped onto my knees next to him, my heart hammering in my ears.

"This must be your dad's, from Vietnam," he said. He rubbed the top of the box with the flat of his hand. "Look," he said, and rocked back on his heels.

There was just one word, and a hand-painted set of numbers written in what looked like red fingernail polish:

SHORT 12̶ 1̶1̶ 1̶0̶ 9̶ 8̶ 7

"What do you think it means?" Stargazer asked. Even though my heart was slamming around in my chest, I thought, *Finally, something Stargazer doesn't know.* But then the rush and roar of the ocean sucking at my legs, wanting to drag me to the bottom of the ocean, came back. I whispered, "We have to put it back."

"Are you crazy?" said Stargazer. "There might be ammo in here. Real ammo."

Number one on the list of forbidden things in Stargazer's trailer was guns, which meant anything connected with violence, war, or killing. His mother was so afraid of hunters and their guns that she made Stargazer and Summer wear bright orange vests outside during deer-hunting season. The fact that there was a hunting club in town—they mostly went after wild pigs and deer—was nearly enough to make her move to the wilds of Alaska. She probably would have, but Beldon said they'd only run into moose and bear hunters there, with even bigger guns.

"Look, the box is locked," Stargazer said. A padlock dangled from an eyebolt screwed into one end, holding the handle shut. "Must be something good in there." He looked around, picked up a fist-sized rock, and started smashing at the lock.

I stood up, took a step backward. At my house, the number one unwritten rule was to honor people's privacy. I was absolutely sure we should not be doing this. The sound of Stargazer's rock smashing down on the lock bounced off the back of the house and the side of the garage. Or at least, we should be doing this somewhere else, where nobody would see.

But I didn't stop him.

Stargazer grunted. "Got it," he said. I knelt next to him. I wanted Stargazer to hurry, to find out what was inside. He pulled open the top. Gauze rolls and bandages. He tipped the box, and they tumbled out onto the ground. I reached inside and pulled out an Ace bandage. Stargazer pulled out several small brown bottles and a pair of scissors.

"This must be what we heard clunking," he said. He waved the scissors over his head, made a few cuts in the air. "Some weapon," he said. "Hold still or I'll cut you to death!"

"Stop it," I said, "before you stab me." I rubbed my throat, felt the tiny scar just above my collarbone. "I'm not kidding." I was suddenly flushed with anger, and somehow afraid. "Put them down right now," I said. "Or I'm going inside."

"Relax, Tracy," he said, looking at me with a worried expression. "They're just for cutting bandages and stuff, not for stabbing people." But he set the scissors carefully on the ground beside him. "Better?"

I nodded, and reached in the ammo box and felt a few more bandages sliding against one another. Why would my dad lock up a bunch of old bandages? Then under them, in one of the corners, I felt a pile of small, slippery pellets. I pulled them out.

It was a chain, just like the chain I wore around my neck for my house key, but a little heavier. A small metal tag dangled from the end.

Stargazer sucked his breath in. "A dogtag," he whispered. "What else is in there?" He stuck his hand in.

My dad's boots suddenly appeared between us.

When I looked up, he was a dark, solid shape against the sky.

"Just what do you kids think you're doing?" he said. His voice was low, dangerous.

Stargazer pulled his hand out.

"We found it," he said. "In the garage. We were just wondering . . ."

"Well, you can quit wondering." He grabbed the chain from my hand. "Put everything back."

We got most of the stuff back in, except for the gauze and Ace bandage. Dad slammed the ammo box shut and stuck it under his arm.

He glared at Stargazer. "This was your idea, wasn't it?"

Stargazer yelped and leaped to his feet.

I jumped up too, scared of the cold, hard anger in Dad's voice, but of something else too. Once I'd seen a skinny dog trapped in the blind end of a dirt alley by a group of boys with sticks and rocks. The dog's teeth were bared, but it cringed, terrified, against a wall. My dad had the same desperate look.

Stargazer crept to his bike and disappeared down the driveway.

Vietnam, Autumn 1974

The moon had gone down and the room was lit only with the flickering kerosene lamp. Cold river mist slipped in the doorway. I pulled the quilt tight around my shoulders. Má was sitting at the table unloading her box, talking to Grandmother.

"From the PX," she said in a low voice as she brought out a can of evaporated milk. "To sell." She pulled out a toothbrush, some bottles of American medicine, two packs of Salem cigarettes, and a bar of soap. "Be careful," she said. "The American GIs say North Vietnamese are coming. There will be a big fight."

Grandmother nodded. "They whisper the same thing at the market." She jumped up from the table and put the milk and medicine on top of the bureau next to our altar for Quan Am. Má handed Grandmother the soap, cigarettes, and toothpaste. Grandmother hid everything in the bottom drawer of the bureau.

Grandmother saw me watching her. "Go back to sleep," she said. "It's dangerous to know too much."

At dinner Dad didn't look angry or desperate anymore, just . . . beat up.

Mom looked from one to the other of us. "What's going on around here?" she asked.

Dad and I said, "Nothing," at exactly the same time.

Mom looked annoyed. "Honestly, you two," she said. "I let my mother rattle on about her committee work and her problems with her housekeeper. I heard all about the boring tea she hosted for the State Department wives. I don't need two sulking people on top of that."

Dad stood up and opened the bottle of bourbon he'd left out on the counter.

Mom slammed her fork down. "What're you doing?" she said to Dad.

"What does it look like," he said, pouring bourbon into his glass. "I'm fixing myself a drink. Then I'm going to go watch TV."

"Fixing yourself *another* drink, you mean," Mom said.

"Fine," said Dad, "*another* drink." He added water, then held his full glass up to Mom in a mock toast, the ice cubes clicking against one another. He took a big swallow, then left the kitchen.

Mom didn't say another word while we finished eating, and neither did I. It was hard to believe just a few hours ago she'd given me a hug.

I cleared our plates while Mom cut three pieces of pie. But when she tried to get Dad to come back to the table for dessert, he yelled over the sound of the TV that he didn't want any. Mom slammed my pie down in front of me so hard the custard and meringue slid halfway off the crust.

"Happy summer, Tracy," she said, and I thought, *What a perfect example of sarcasm.* Mrs. McNally had tried to teach us about sarcasm earlier in the year, but it hadn't made sense to me. Probably, Mrs. McNally said, I didn't understand because I was foreign and English wasn't my native tongue.

But this time I got it. Mom's words said one thing and her voice another.

~

Even in my bed, from all the way across the living room, I heard my parents arguing in their room. Dad's voice was a low drone, Mom's was high and sharp. Why had the ammo box upset my dad so much? Why had it upset me? I'd never even seen it before.

As far as I could remember, anyway.

Lying in the dark, listening, winds stirred through the empty place inside of me.

I lay awake a long time after the arguing stopped.

In the morning I swam up from sleep, like a fish heading for the silvery surface of the water. Did I sleep through my dad knocking on my window when he left for work? I thought about the sound of his feet, the way he would walk lightly across the gravel, the truck door slamming, tires crunching in the gravel as he pulled out. Was that today, or had it been Saturday?

Mom appeared in my bedroom doorway wearing her brown smock, her keys in her hand. "Tracy?" she said. "You awake?" I wondered if Dad had told her about how Stargazer and I had found the ammo box, busted the lock off.

"Dad just called. He forgot to make his lunch. Would you put something together and run it over to him? I'm already late."

"Um-hum," I said. She walked out of the room, then stuck her head back in. I could see tired blue smudges under her eyes. "Remember, his lunch break's at eleven thirty."

"I know," I said. Suddenly I didn't want Mom to just disappear, carelessly, like it was no big deal to leave me alone all day.

Mom must have picked up something, because she asked, "You sure you're going to be all right?"

My first Monday with no school, no Y camp. I sure didn't want to just sit around the house all day.

But the second her worry showed, my feelings rushed back the other way.

"I'll be fine," I said. "Stargazer and I are going to start the ship today. At his place." I wasn't used to lying to Mom. It was amazingly easy.

"Good." She seemed relieved I was going to be at Stargazer's.

"Besides, look," I said. I pulled my key chain out from under my pajama top. "Got my key. I'm ready for summer."

"Okay," she said. "Have fun at Stargazer's." She closed my bedroom door.

I tucked my key back inside my top and jumped out of bed.

Vietnam, Spring 1975

Grandmother stood on the rear deck of her wooden canoe. She rocked forward on her feet and pushed on the long oar handles. I lay on my stomach on the front deck, trailing my fingers in the muddy river, letting the morning sun soak into my shirt. Grandmother had woken me before dawn, three baskets of smoked fish already stacked in the middle of the canoe. A few more hours of rowing and we'd be at the mountain people's village, where Grandmother could sell the fish.

Suddenly Grandmother took in a sharp breath. I sat up and followed her look. Another flat-bottomed canoe had shot out from the bushes overhanging the river and was heading straight for us. There were three men, two squatting in front, one standing in back, pushing hard on the oars. Even from here I could see their clothes were patched and faded.

Grandmother muttered a quick prayer to Quan Am for our safety as she rowed evenly, with no hurry, as if the soldiers had no business with us and would pass us by. "Vietcong," she whispered to me. She tipped her chin at the quilt rolled up in the middle of the boat. Fighting the Americans under Ho Chi Minh—the leader they called Uncle Ho—they would not like my con lai face.

I inched toward the middle of the boat. When it wasn't safe, Grandmother had me curl up on the bottom, covered with the quilt. But it was too late now. They had already seen me.

The soldiers headed straight for us, matching strokes with Grandmother, gaining on us fast. I could see that the soldier in the middle with a long, thin mustache held an AK-47 across his chest.

They drew up next to us and the soldier in front grabbed the edge of our canoe and pulled, until the sides of our boats scraped and we rose and fell together on the swells.

"Where are you headed today?" the first soldier asked Grandmother. His cheeks were hollow, his eyes feverish as if he had malaria, but his words were respectful.

"Up to the mountain people's village," she said, her voice carefully even.

"What do you have in the baskets?" he asked. He stared at the three baskets stacked on top of each other, next to the quilt.

I could see the soldier was hungry. He could probably even smell the fish. Behind him, the middle soldier leaned forward. He leered at me, stroked the butt of his rifle.

"Uncle Ho has many of us to feed as we fight for freedom," the first soldier said. "With so much chemical spraying by the American planes, the rice grows big but never ripens."

Grandmother nodded. We had the same problem in our village. "American rice," we called it.

"We have come from far away," the soldier continued. "I'm sure you would like to help feed Uncle Ho's hungry soldiers."

Grandmother was trapped. "I am always honored to help Uncle Ho," she said. She squatted down and opened the top basket. The middle soldier leaned forward, flipped the lid back on the basket. "There are others back in the jungle," he said, and pulled all three baskets into their canoe. "Many others."

There was nothing she could do.

Dad was totally wrong if he thought he could just shove the ammo box on some shelf and life would go on like before. Didn't he understand it was too late for that? Something had been trapped in the box—maybe hopes and dreams and fears—and now they were out and blowing around us, skittering between us all. I wanted to look through the box again, feel the dogtag, read the labels on the little bottles. Maybe it was my hopes and dreams, and Dad's fear. I couldn't tell. It was all tangled up.

Knowing no one would disturb me, the first place I headed was the garage. I checked every shelf, and looked behind his stacks of paint cans. I pulled a six-foot ladder over from the tool corner and got up to the high shelves crammed with old junk. I found the seat from my old swing set. A round aquarium for the goldfish Dad had won for me at the May fair by tossing pennies into a glass jar. My mom's canning supplies. A heavy black telephone with a rotary dial. Big flakes of sawdust covered everything, stuck on with grimy dust.

Inside the house I checked behind Dad's chair, the couch. I looked under the kitchen sink, through every cupboard in the back laundry room.

Finally I stood in the doorway of my parents' room,

unsure if I should look there. Mom's sense of privacy was so strong, she'd even bring my backpack to me if she needed to borrow a pen rather than go through it herself.

I sucked in a breath and walked in. I had to know. I had to see that ammo box again, and the small metal tag on the chain.

Nothing under the bed. I ran my hands all the way to the back of the closet floor, but only found my mom's flats and one pair of heels, an old pair of my dad's boots, and his shiny black dress shoes. I pulled a chair in from the living room and stood on it in front of the closet. It was unlikely my dad would put something as filthy as the ammo box up here on the shelf but just in case, I pulled aside sweaters and extra blankets to check. Nothing.

Where could my dad have put it? I stood on the chair and stared at their bed. It was as neat and tidy as always, the pillows soft round lumps under the heavy golden bedspread. The numbers on the digital clock on the nightstand made a tiny click as they flipped over to 11:00.

A quick knock on the front door made me jump and almost fall off the chair.

When I answered, it was Stargazer.

"What're you doing here?" I asked. He always came around to the back.

"I knocked on the back door, but you didn't hear me," he whispered. "But I saw your bike, so I knew you were here." He stuck his head in and looked behind me. "Your dad's truck's in the lumberyard, so I figured it was safe to come over." Stargazer would have ridden right past Jones Brothers on his way here.

"If you knew my dad was at work, why are you whispering?" I said.

He shrugged. "Your mom's gone too, right?" he whispered.

I nodded.

"Let's go look for the ammo box." He was still whispering. He slipped in the door and closed it behind him. Even in the dusky hall light, I could see his eyes were full of excitement.

"You can quit whispering," I said, louder than I meant to. My voice bounced off the tile floor in the entry hall. He was beginning to bug me, casing my house like he was planning a stakeout, only looking for the ammo box because it was about war and killing. He didn't feel the ghosts of Vietnam that had been trapped in there, the ghosts we'd let out yesterday.

Stargazer followed me through the living room and into the kitchen. "I've got to make lunch and take it to my dad," I said. "Right now," I added as he opened his mouth to protest. I didn't feel like telling Stargazer I'd already been over every inch of the garage and house, and the box was gone.

ॐ

I pulled up on my bike in front of the store and flipped down the kickstand.

"I'll wait out here for you," Stargazer said. I didn't blame him. I knew he didn't want to risk running into my dad. Dad's blue Chevy was right there in the parking lot next to a rusty white stepside, two trucks with "Jones Brothers" written on the side, and a couple of others. A forklift pulled out of the wide doors of the warehouse, carrying a stack of two-by-fours. It wasn't my dad driving; it was Frank, the other guy who worked in the yard.

I slipped inside the store with my dad's lunch, the buzzer making an irritating *zzzt* sound. There were three people in line at the back counter. Mr. Conner was sitting on his high stool next to the cash register. His lips moved as he added up a row of numbers he'd penciled on the back of a brown paper bag.

I tried to peer around the guys in line to catch Mr. Conner's eye, but he didn't look up. The big wall clock behind him said 11:32. Close enough. An office door behind Mr. Conner was open. Mr. Jones was sitting at his desk, talking on the phone, oblivious to the long line.

I checked to see if there were any new signs stapled up on the wall while I waited, but it was just the ones I'd read plenty of times before.

NO SHIRT, NO SHOES, NO SERVICE. Stargazer had told me the sign was really meant for restaurants, but Jones Brothers was antihippie. He said Beldon wouldn't shop there if he could go anywhere else.

AMERICA, LOVE IT OR LEAVE IT.

Also antihippie, Stargazer said. I wasn't sure what it meant. How could you just *leave*?

DON'T EVEN THINK ABOUT ASKING FOR CREDIT IF YOU'RE DRUNK. Stargazer said that was antiredneck. If it was for hippies, it would say DON'T EVEN THINK ABOUT ASKING FOR CREDIT IF YOU'RE STONED. Which, Stargazer said, would be equally stupid, because who can think if they are drunk or stoned?

Finally there was just one man left. I could see he was a carpenter by the tape measure clipped to his back pocket and his dirty work boots. He dropped a couple of utility knives, a mud tray, and five rolls of tape on the counter.

"I thought Fred picked up the supplies," said Mr. Conner. "Why'd he send you?"

I held Dad's lunch up and waved it back and forth. I could tell Mr. Conner saw me, but he pretended he didn't, just kept figuring numbers on a new bag.

"We're behind on the framing," the carpenter said. "Fred was nailing off a two-by-four and shot a galvanized nail right between his thumb and index finger. Had me pull it out and kept on working. But his hand's swollen up like a tick today."

Now the clock behind the counter said 11:45. I hoped my dad was too busy out in the yard to be wondering where his lunch was.

"He's one tough nut," said Mr. Conner, shaking his head. "I had a lieutenant like him in the army."

Mr. Conner was so old, I'd never thought about him being in the military. I knew he'd been a cowboy when he was young. When he walked, he kind of limped along, and you could see daylight between his knees. "Broke plenty of horses," he liked to say, "and a couple broke me."

"You can bet Fred's in a nasty mood today," the carpenter said while Mr. Conner loaded his stuff into a bag. "He hates to even strap on his tool belt, but we were short a guy, and he was working with the rest of us. Then this happens."

Short a guy? Short seven guys? I wondered, thinking about my dad's ammo box.

Was that what Stargazer had uncovered on the box? Was somebody filling up a crew of twelve?

I spun around and glanced out the window at Stargazer standing by his bike. He was staring intently at me, and gave me a frustrated "can't you hurry up" look.

The carpenter finally grabbed his stuff off the counter and headed out the door.

I put my dad's lunch on the counter.

"Hi there, Monkey," said Mr. Conner. One of the first times I went to visit my dad I ran out the swinging doors to the yard to find him. Nobody was allowed in the warehouse or out in the yard, but I didn't know it. Mr. Conner chased after me and grabbed me just before a yard guy backing up a forklift ran over me. Afterward, Mr. Conner said I clung to him like a monkey, which I probably did.

"What can I do for you?" he asked, his voice booming across the empty store.

"Can you give this to my dad?" I said.

"Sure," said Mr. Conner.

I glanced behind me. Nobody waiting. I'd never really talked to Mr. Conner before.

"Mr. Conner?"

"That's me."

"So, you were in the army?"

"Yep."

"In Vietnam?" The ghosts whispered in the air around me.

"Nope. I'm too old. Korea." I'd have to ask Stargazer about Korea.

"Did you have an ammo box?"

"All soldiers do."

He didn't seem surprised I was asking him questions.

"You gotta have ammo if you want to shoot and not get shot, Monkey," he added.

"What does it mean when somebody writes 'SHORT' on their ammo box, and then numbers? Does that mean running short of ammo? Short of people?"

He pushed a brown paper bag across the counter to me. "Show me what you mean."

I drew the rectangular top of the ammo box, then "SHORT" and the list of numbers I'd seen in red nail polish. The door buzzer went off. I shoved the bag back toward Mr. Conner. It suddenly seemed important he tell me quickly, while we were alone, not with somebody standing behind me listening.

"Ah," he said. "Short on time. Once you know you're going home soon, you become short on days somebody can try to kill you. You start counting every day, every hour, you want to make it home so bad."

I glanced over my shoulder and saw Stargazer peering around the edge of the hardware aisle. His eyes were wide open, like he'd just figured out what we were talking about.

Mr. Conner laughed. "We had a lot of ways of joking about it. 'I'm so short, I need a ladder to tie my shoes.' 'I'm so short, the rats don't even bother me. I just walk right under them.'"

I leaned across the counter to write on the bag, hoping Stargazer would stay right where he was and not butt in. "Why would the numbers be crossed off like this"—I showed him—"and only go down to seven?" Too late. Stargazer was right behind me, breathing on my neck.

The smile fell off Mr. Conner's face and he looked suddenly serious. "Don't ask an old soldier that, Monkey. We're way too superstitious."

He twisted around on his stool and yelled through the open doorway to the yard. "Bob, Monkey's here with your lunch!"

He shoved the paper bag across the counter at me. "Ask your dad."

I didn't say the obvious: my dad was an old soldier too.

"Ask me what?" My dad appeared in the doorway.

"Nothing," I said. I slid the paper off the counter, down where he couldn't see it.

I pushed the lunch box toward Dad. "I made you two peanut butter sandwiches," I said quickly. "And the last Coke in the fridge, it's in here too." Maybe if I kept talking I could change the subject.

The door buzzed and my dad shot a quick glance at it. I twisted around and saw Stargazer jump on his bike, pedaling even before he was in the seat. That made it twice in two days he'd run from my dad.

"She wants to know what 'short' means," said Mr. Conner.

Dad stepped back like he'd been slapped, then

leaned across the counter and said in a low voice, "Short is what your little hippie friend is gonna be in our family if he doesn't get his nose out of my business. Both of you knock it off. Got it?"

I nodded.

Vietnam, Spring 1975

The soldier in the middle of the canoe grinned at me. "Who's this round-eyed one?" he asked Grandmother. He ran his dirty fingers down my cheek. His armpit stunk of old sweat and too many nights sleeping on the ground in his clothes.

"She's only con lai," said Grandmother. "I try to make her work hard for me, but she is lazy, like her no-good father." She shifted forward, trying to edge her body between me and the solider, but he blocked her with his arm.

"We could teach her to work hard," he said, and wrapped his hand around the back of my neck.

"I will beat it into her myself," Grandmother said. She stepped forward, grabbed my shirt, and pushed me down onto the bottom of the canoe.

I knew she wanted me out of reach, where the soldier

couldn't sweep me off the front of the boat with one arm and row away with me.

"Maybe you don't beat her hard enough," he said.

He reached for me again, and grabbed a handful of my hair. "Such light hair. The enemy is inside her, just as he is in our country." His wispy mustache hung over his top lip, mixed with the dried spit caked in the corners of his mouth.

"I will beat the American out of her," Grandmother said. She was talking fast, telling them anything so they would leave me alone. "Soon her hair will be dark. Now go, take your fish, and leave an old woman to deal with her troubles alone."

"She's right," the first soldier said. "Let's go eat the fish before we have to share with too many others."

The soldier let go of my hair, reached behind me, and snatched Grandmother's knife from the bottom of the canoe. He felt the sharp tip, and nodded.

Grandmother drew in a short breath. The soldier grunted, dropped the knife in the top basket with the fish, and sat back on his heels.

"Quickly," Grandmother whispered to me.

I scuttled backward like a crab and wedged myself into the far side of the boat. Grandmother pulled back on one *oar, forward on the other, and turned us back the way we'd come. Her hands trembled on the oars.*

I biked up to Stargazer's and found him in the trailer sitting with Summer at the table. Beldon was home, making lunch. Summer was drawing with a set of broken crayons, and Stargazer was making a list in his notebook.

"Where's Ruthie?" I asked.

"She took my truck over to Ukiah to see the midwife," Beldon said. "We're about to have lunch. You hungry?" He didn't wait for an answer, but just grabbed the cheese that was out and started cutting more slices.

I scooted into a seat across from Summer and Stargazer. Stargazer wrote something on his list with a pencil, then stared out the window, tapping the pencil on the table.

"What're you listing?"

"Animals by the river," he said.

This was like the opposite of making a mark for every shooting star he saw. I knew that when Stargazer thought something bad was going to happen, he started making a list. He'd made one last year of edible fruits and berries, and then Beldon fell off a ladder pruning the apple trees and broke his ankle. Stargazer said that if he could see the order of things by making a list, he figured he'd know how to deal with the problem when it came.

I didn't think it was very scientific, but Stargazer said the first rule of science was observation. That didn't make sense, but I figured it was just one of those Stargazer things.

"Like what kinds of animals?" I asked.

"I saw mosquito fish. Water skeeters. Grasshoppers. Dragonflies."

Summer looked up from her page of blue and red scribbles. "Bunnies?" she asked.

"No, no bunnies," Stargazer said. He'd convinced Summer there were rabbits in the woods, but she never had seen one.

"No bunnies?" she asked again, looking disappointed.

"Nope," said Stargazer. "They're hiding in soft nests under the trees so the owls don't catch them."

He tapped his list with a pencil. "And I listed all the animals I couldn't see that were probably hiding and watching me. Tree frogs. Deer. Wild turkeys. Water snakes. There're a lot of animals out there, you know."

"Like bunnies," Summer said.

"Right," said Stargazer. "I'll put them on my list."

"Owls," she said, and stuck her thumb in her mouth.

I put my head next to his and whispered in his ear so Summer wouldn't hear. "What's the bad thing?"

"I don't know yet," he whispered back.

I didn't tell Stargazer what my dad said, leaning over the counter at the hardware store while Stargazer was pumping hard up the road to his house. But maybe Stargazer had felt it. The ammo box held secrets that could rip me and Stargazer apart.

Vietnam, Spring 1975

Grandmother slid the boat into the water palms overhanging the riverbank. Her eyes flitted up and down the river, watching for more trouble as the shadows lengthened on the water. I longed to leap out of the boat and run beside the river. I'd run so fast I'd only hear the wind in my ears. I wouldn't listen for the American helicopters, dropping low and spitting bullets from machine guns. I wouldn't listen for the drone of their big planes, dropping bombs that made the sound of a rice-threshing machine as they fell.

I didn't want to keep watching for trip mines and sharpened bamboo stakes in covered pits hidden by the Vietcong just waiting for an American GI to come by.

"They took your knife," I said to Grandmother.

"A small price to pay for keeping you safe," she said,

and spat over the side of the canoe, as if even thinking of the Vietcong made a bad taste in her mouth.

I fell asleep, still curled into a tight ball. I woke up with Grandmother shaking my shoulder. "When the sun is down, we'll go back and see if they left the baskets. Now we'll stay hidden, like small crayfish do when the catfish searches in the mud with his whiskers, looking for something to eat. Too many Vietcong," she said, "dangerous." But her voice was sad.

I knew she was thinking of her third son, Luc, who'd run away to the north to join Ho Chi Minh's army before the South Vietnamese Army could draft him. Grandmother had been called in for interrogation by the South Vietnamese after he left. They brought her home on the back of a motorcycle, and dumped her in the front yard. I rushed out to meet her, just as she fell to her knees.

I ran next door to Yen's for help but she stayed inside, too afraid to come out. "For once," she said, "having the face of the enemy is your protection. They know your mother is friendly with the Americans. They won't bother you." She boiled a pot of black tea and ladled in two spoonfuls of sugar. I carried a cup out to Grandmother. She drank sip after sip, then slowly crawled into the house.

After dark Yen slipped quietly through our door. She

pulled off Grandmother's bloody clothes and washed her bruised body. I sat against the wall in the flickering light from the kerosene lamp and watched, terrified. "I said nothing, nothing," Grandmother groaned. "This war will kill us all before it is over."

Yen hushed her, but Grandmother's words, held back so tight during the interrogation, spilled out of her mouth. "What will happen to me?" she asked, like a small child. "Husband and first son dead in the fighting. Second son drafted and far away, third son run off to fight with Ho Chi Minh. First daughter in Saigon, and second daughter bringing shame on the family with an American man. Who will tend my grave when I die? Who will save me from being a wandering ghost?"

The next morning I got up as soon as my dad tapped on the window. I didn't want to think about the ammo box and the dogtag anymore. I wanted the ghosts just to leave me alone. If I didn't think of them, didn't leave a hollowed-out place for them in my belly, maybe they'd disappear. Maybe if we got going on the Viking funeral ship, some of Stargazer's enthusiasm would rub off on me.

The morning sun hadn't burned the dew off the

plants when I arrived at Stargazer's. I leaned my bike against the side of the trailer. Jip and Pixie bolted out from under it, barking and yipping and wriggling. Halfway down to the river I could see Beldon in the garden on his hands and knees throwing something into a big basket beside him.

The dogs ran in with me and nearly knocked Ruthie over. She was at the kitchen counter, leaning way over her big belly to stir something in a bowl. Summer was in her favorite white nightgown with eyelet trim, lying on top of the covers with Stargazer on their table-turned-bed. Summer was sucking her thumb and listening to Stargazer tell her some kind of animal story.

I waited for him to pause, and then interrupted him, because when he told a story, he could go on a long time.

"Let's build the biggest, most beautiful Viking funeral ship that's ever been launched," I said.

He stopped talking and looked at me in surprise. "That's more than we can do," he said. "And besides, we'd have to have slaves captured in Ireland to sacrifice."

"Very funny," I said. It was always a little weird how

much Stargazer would inhale about a subject when he was interested. "You know what I mean. The best *replica* ever built." I said "rep-li-ca" the way the docent at the Natural History Museum had said it when we took a school trip there. "This is an im-port-ant-life-sized-rep-li-ca," she'd said as we stood around the ship in the big hall. "But smaller than the one we saw," I added.

Then what Stargazer had said sunk in.

"Really?" I asked. "They sacrificed slaves?"

"Don't you read anything?" said Stargazer. He always trailed behind everyone else when we went on museum field trips, reading every word of those boring labels they put by each exhibition. "The king needed everything for his afterlife, so they killed horses and sheep, and slaves. There's even a queen buried in a big ship in Norway with a slave beside her."

"That's gross," I said.

"Tell my story!" demanded Summer.

"Hey," he said, "we could sacrifice Summer. We'll tummy-gummy her to death."

He twisted around and reached for her. She started shrieking and laughing before he even got his face on her stomach and started in with big raspberries. Both the dogs leaped to their feet and started yipping, and Ruthie threw up her hands. "Dogs out!" she yelled, shoving open the door and pushing them out. The trailer shook as they bolted down the stairs together.

I knew Summer could be a pain, but right that minute, watching her tussle on the bed with Stargazer, I wished I had a little sister. I wished this was my family: a big, fun-loving, shrieking, yelling family with two dogs and another baby on the way, and a mother who made herbal teas, even if it meant I would have to live in a trailer. Even if I had to share a bed with all of the other kids.

"Enough," yelled Ruthie. "Put up the table, Stargazer. Tracy, help Summer get dressed, okay? Her clothes are in the bottom dresser drawer in our room."

Beldon burst in the door, carrying a big basket. He dropped it on the floor beside Ruthie. "Heavy sucker," he said.

"Umm . . . ," he said to Ruthie. "Smells delicious." He wrapped his arms around her belly from the back and kissed her on the neck.

"Take it easy, buster," she said, and shrugged him off, but it was easy to see she liked it.

"Go sit down," he said. "I just have time to get these cooked before I head out for work."

When I came back out of the bedroom with Summer in her favorite overalls (dirty, she won) and a T-shirt (clean, I won), Stargazer had put up the table and set five places. Beldon had a stack of pancakes steaming on the counter.

Even though I'd already had a bowl of cereal, I slid in next to Summer. Beldon put two big pancakes on my plate.

While we ate, I tried to figure out what all the smells were in the trailer. The sweet jammy huckleberry pancakes mixed with slightly burned butter on my plate. But there was also dogs and dirt, the river, and the tang of Ruthie's herbs from yesterday's batch of tea lingering in the air. All together it made the most comforting smell I could think of.

Between bites, Stargazer drew out his plans for how we were going to build the ship. He'd realized that for us to do it without any adults, we needed to figure out an easier way. Because we wanted it to burn, he thought we should use a cardboard box, supported on two thin logs to keep it out of the water as long as possible.

He jumped up and cleared his place, then picked up his notebook and turned to a new page. "Here's how we'll make the sail and dragon's head," he said, drawing them with a pencil. For the first time, I really listened.

Vietnam, Spring 1975

Grandmother's round face, so close to mine, her hands on my shoulders, voice murmuring like the river. "This time I go alone. Too many soldiers. I'll be back home tomorrow, if it is the will of the ancestors."

I understood. A day and a night, to row against the current, to take smoked fish and sell them to the mountain people. Rowing downstream far enough for safety, sliding beneath the overhanging water palms to sleep. One more morning to glide back home on the river current.

Grandmother touched my hair. She smelled of gutted fish and charcoal smoke. "What cannot be changed, must be endured, granddaughter." Then, like smoke, she was gone.

Over the next week, Stargazer and I fell into a routine. I'd get to his place early—early enough for a second breakfast—and we'd head out to Beldon's shop and work on the ship. After cutting just the right length logs, we set a big cardboard box on them.

"Why don't we just make a raft?" I asked. "At least it would be flat."

"We're not making the Kon-Tiki," he said.

I didn't ask what that was, but he told me anyway.

"It's a raft. This Norwegian guy made one out of balsa wood logs and rope. In 1947 he sailed from South America to the Polynesian islands. Like some people from an ancient civilization had."

"Why?" I asked him.

"To prove a long voyage could have been done without any modern equipment, long before Columbus."

Another bit of Stargazer-only information.

"Plus, we need sides to hang the shields on," Stargazer said, "and a dragon's head at the prow, and—"

"Okay, okay," I interrupted him.

We lashed the box onto the logs with gaffer's tape Beldon had left over from when he used to work for a rock band and had to tape down electrical cords so that hundreds of dancing people wouldn't trip on them.

Then we painted the whole thing with enamel

paint, which Stargazer said would waterproof the boat if we did it a couple of times.

In the afternoons we went swimming in the river and shivered and burned on the hot rocks, and Stargazer told me all his plans for the sails and rigging and shields. Except for the shields, he wanted everything made out of something that would burn. And we set a date: the night of the August full moon. No adults invited. It would just be the two of us. Stargazer told me all about how the moon would look really big and close to the earth due to "atmospheric phenomenon." I had no idea where he'd learned that, but mostly I wondered how we were going to sneak out in the middle of the night to launch the ship.

I noticed Stargazer was still carrying his notebook everywhere, and I'd see him looking for new animals to put in. He wandered around the garden one afternoon, and added spiders, earthworms, grubs, cabbage moths, and stink beetles. On another page he drew a picture of the ammo box, and one of the dogtag.

One day on the river rocks I asked, "What are dogtags for?"

"All soldiers wear one. It's got your name on it, and

your blood type, so if you need blood when you get shot they can give it to you in a hurry."

He reached out and touched his notebook. He didn't say anything else, and I didn't either.

᠅

When my mind wandered back to the ammo box, or the dogtag, or *there*, I'd say to myself, "*Leave it alone.*"

It worked in the daytime. But nights were different. In my restless nights, I dreamed of the hungry ghosts that had surged out of the ammo box when we opened it, ghosts that wanted to eat my father up from the inside, and tear me apart from Stargazer.

Two weeks after we found the ammo box I woke up with the blankets and sheets twisted around my waist. My room was completely dark, but I felt crowded, afraid, like someone was watching me. Far up the street a dog barked. Then silence. I stared into the darkness and saw it all again in slow motion, like a series of slides projected onto the ceiling: My dad standing over Stargazer and me as we crouched by the ammo box. Grabbing the chain from me. Slamming the box shut and putting it under his arm. His hand sliding into his pocket, coming out empty.

He put the chain and dogtag in his pocket,

Leave it alone . . .

not in the ammo box.

Leave it alone. The ghosts sighed and whispered around me, pressed in.

I pulled the covers up to my neck, licked the sweat off my upper lip. I rolled over, making sure the covers stayed up to my neck, even though I was hot, and stared at the window. The first glimmers of dawn were already gathering outside. The light slowly brightened the window, outlining the four panes. I heard my parents get up, smelled coffee brewing. The back door closed softly, and my father's footsteps crunched on the gravel. He knocked on the window.

"Morning, chickadee," he said, but it sounded like someone's voice on a tape recorder, like he didn't want the morning, didn't want to go to work, didn't want anything but to be left alone.

Vietnam, Spring 1975

The light from the lamp flickered and threw shadows on the wall. It gutted down, flared up again. The sharp smell of kerosene mixed with the sweet smoke of incense burning on someone's nearby altar, and the dampness from the river. The flame flickered up again, went out.

Are you safe, Grandmother, hidden in the water palms, wrapped in the quilt, your new knife near you for protection?

In the quiet, cicadas thrummed, and a hunting owl called cu-cu. I felt my way in the darkness to the bed and unrolled the quilt on top. I sat cross-legged on the quilt, listened to the tree frogs. "Quan Am," I whispered into the darkness, "keep Grandmother safe, keep me safe."

But I could feel them outside, the lost wandering ghosts, the villagers and soldiers killed in battle. They were hanging upside down in the trees, shuffling along the paths. They

knew I was in here, alone and scared. I put my back to the
wall, pulled the quilt tight around me.

As soon as my mother left, I headed into the living
room. I looked under all the furniture, and felt behind
the books on the bookshelf, my fingers trailing through
a thin layer of dust. If Mom knew there was dust back
there, she'd probably take every book off the shelf and
wash it down with bleach.

On the middle shelf were my books from long ago.
Grandee used to send me what she called "essential
classics for a well-read child." *Charlotte's Web. A Tree
Grows in Brooklyn*. A whole set of Laura Ingalls Wilder.
I pulled down *By the Banks of Plum Creek*.

At night my dad would read to me. One chapter, or
two, even three, if I begged him to keep reading. Then
he'd close the book and say, "Time to sleep. Rooster's
going to wake you up in the morning." I'd reach up and
pat Dad's back. "Night, Rooster," I would say. On Dad's
back, right between his shoulder blades, was a blue tat-
too of a rooster, wings spread wide, neck stretched out
as he crowed. "Good night, my little chickadee," my dad
would say in his gruff rooster voice.

I slid the book back on the shelf and headed into

the kitchen. I sat in my seat at the table and stared at all the cabinets, top and bottom. At first I thought how long it would take for me to check them all, then I realized he wouldn't hide anything here. This was my mother's territory, not his.

If he hid the dogtag, that is. If he didn't throw it into the ocean, reaching into his pocket to send the chain twisting and spinning into the water after first hefting up the ammo box and sending the ghosts to a watery grave, hoping they couldn't escape.

For a moment my image of him at the ocean was so strong I was sure it was a waste of time to look any further. I shook my head, to knock out what I was thinking. Maybe, but maybe not.

I headed to my parents' bedroom and looked through the nightstand on my father's side of the bed. Nothing. I moved quickly, feeling somehow this was even more wrong, more personal, than looking for the ammo box.

In the closet I picked up all my dad's shoes, shook them to see if anything would fall out, felt underneath each one. Still nothing.

I'd gone in my dad's dresser drawers many times, putting away clothes, but this was different. I checked the pockets of his pants, front and back, without unfolding them, then put them back in a tidy stack. I felt around and under all his T-shirts.

His underwear drawer. Of course. That's where I stashed things. Like the saltwater taffy I used to sneak, one piece at a time, from a big barrel at Redwood Cove Market. I never ate it, just stuck it under my socks and underwear at the very back of the drawer. Or the ring with the shiny blue stone that I found in second grade in the girls' bathroom by one of the faucets. Even after our teacher read a bulletin from the principal's office asking anyone who saw it to return it, I didn't.

My fingers slid over a slick piece of paper in my dad's underwear drawer. I snagged under a corner with my thumbnail and pulled it out.

It was a photo of three guys in white T-shirts and camouflage pants. Short hair. The one in the middle was my dad. He was skinnier, and younger, with a mustache, like in the wedding picture on the wall of the living room. I looked closer. At first his eyes looked like he was smiling, but then I realized his eyes were crinkled up like the light was too bright. He looked serious, reserved. Standing next to him was a guy a few inches shorter, grinning, with glasses. One hand rested on a helmet lashed onto the top of a heavy-looking backpack next to him. On my dad's other side was a tall, muscular guy. Rolled up in one sleeve was a small square packet, in his fingers a half-smoked cigarette.

I flipped it over. "You, me, and Bluto" was scrawled on the back in pencil. "Da Nang, 1968."

I heard the front door shut and nearly jumped out of my skin. I shoved the photo back in the drawer, turned, and ran.

I slammed right into Stargazer in the front hall.

He yelped and threw his arms up around his head.

"What're you doing here?" I yelled, louder than I meant to, I was so relieved.

"Jeez, Tracy!" he said, dropping his hands by his side. "I thought you were your dad."

"I thought you might be my dad too!" I blurted out.

We stared at each other. His chest was heaving in and out.

"What's up?" he said suspiciously.

I shrugged. I wanted to tell Stargazer but I didn't want him to know I was sneaking through my parents' drawers. Not that he would think there was anything strange about it. At his house, there was no such thing as privacy. "We're a family who shares," Beldon said whenever Stargazer tried to keep something away from Summer. When I gave him a paint set for his birthday last year, he'd hidden it out by the chicken coop so that Summer didn't get into it and mess it all up.

"What're you doing here?" I asked again.

"The door was unlocked," he said.

"So?"

He shrugged. "So I let myself in." They never locked the door of their trailer, and Stargazer thought it was weird I had to lock and unlock my front door to go in and out.

"We've got to get the last coat of paint on the ship so it can dry," he said. "I came to get you. I could see your dad's truck was gone . . . I thought it would be safe to come in." He laughed. Not a funny laugh, but a relieved laugh. "At least, I thought it was safe until you body-slammed me." He punched me in the shoulder, a little too hard.

"So . . . what's up?" he asked.

I considered for a moment, decided I would tell him.

"I was looking for something," I said.

His eyes got wide. "Did you find the ammo box?" He looked over my shoulder like he expected to see it sitting right on their bed.

I shook my head.

He rocked back on his heels, disappointed.

"But I did find a photo," I said.

"Of what?" he asked.

I waved for him to follow me into my parents' room, and fished out the photo.

"This," I whispered, even though I knew I didn't need to whisper.

He took the photo from me and held it by the edges. For a few long seconds he didn't say anything, just stared at it.

"Look at all that ammo," he finally said.

I peered over his shoulder.

"They're for an M-60 machine gun," Stargazer explained. "The ammunition comes in hundred-round belts, like these."

Didn't Stargazer realize this wasn't about ammo? "Look," I said, and pointed. "It's my dad."

"Hey!" he said, like he hadn't even heard me. His elbow dug into my ribs. "There's an ammo box."

I looked carefully at the photo. Long, heavy-looking rows of machine gun ammo crisscrossed the lumpy-looking backpack. Hanging on one side was a canteen, and tied to the back of the pack was a gun, the barrel jutting up above the helmet. Strapped to the bottom of the backpack was an ammo box, nearly hidden by the trailing ends of the machine gun bullets.

"Do you think it's the same one?" Stargazer asked.

I snatched the photo from him. "We better put it back," I said. Why didn't he understand this was about people alive, and maybe people dead, and why I was here? Didn't he get it?

Vietnam, Spring 1975

Grandmother didn't come back. I unwrapped the two rice balls she'd left me—rice and beans wrapped in green banana leaves—and ate them, first one, then the other.

The next day I collected small crabs from the shallow river edge. Overhead, black clouds pushed into the sky. The river turned choppy in the wind and snapped at my ankles.

I put the crabs in a small metal basin and sat on the bed and dreamed. When Grandmother came back, we'd go to the market for soft noodles and vegetables. I'd gather snails from the rice paddies and we'd make a rich soup flavored with fish sauce.

Hunger tore at my stomach, and made me dizzy and afraid. I slipped outside only to look up the river for Grandmother's canoe, and to walk quickly across the swaying *monkey bridge to use the outhouse. The river, angry and deep brown with mud, heaved and swelled as the sky darkened.*

At the end of the day I heard shouts and calls as people returned home from the rice fields and the market. I could tell they were hurrying, eager to get inside before the storm. Wind rustled the palm frond roof, and brought in the smell of the neighbor's charcoal smoke, and peppers and scallions frying in pork fat.

I found the banana leaves I'd tossed outside, and licked and chewed them, getting off the last half-dried grains of salty rice.

That night I brought a giant zucchini back from Stargazer's. Mom and I made a stuffing out of rice and ground beef and Hamburger Helper. The whole time we were working together she was humming quietly.

"What?" I asked her. But she only smiled and said, "You'll see."

Dad took an extra-long shower, fixed himself a drink, and sat in the living room watching the six o'clock news. When Mom called him for dinner, he slipped into his seat without saying anything to either of us. What were the ghosts whispering to him? Could he hear them right now? I thought of the photo of Bluto and "me" and the backpacks with the ammo boxes strapped underneath. Who were Bluto and "me," anyway? Did the ghosts weave in and out of their dreams too?

Suddenly I felt sorry for Dad. He looked so beat-up.

Mom looked at him, and some of the light went out of her eyes. She served the food, then said lightly, "I've got some good news."

Dad looked up.

"I got a raise today."

"Really," said Dad. He put down his fork. "How much?"

"Another twenty cents an hour," she said, grinning. "But that's not the best part."

Dad raised his eyebrows. "Well?" he said.

"It's retroactive to April first." She jumped up, grabbed her purse off the counter, and pulled out a piece of paper. "Look! My pay stub." She waved it over her head. "I got a check for the past due and already put it in the bank."

"I'll drink to that," said Dad. Mom and I both watched him as he poured himself a new drink.

Mom squeezed her lips together, then stiffened her

shoulders, like she wasn't going to let his mood get to her. She turned to me.

"I've got tomorrow off," said Mom. "What do you say, Tracy—want to go on a secret errand with me tomorrow?"

♪

The next morning I was up and dressed before Mom got out of bed. I could hear her showering while I ate a piece of toast with peanut butter and strawberry jam.

I was finished by the time she made it to the kitchen, blinking in the light. "Ready," I said.

"Coffee first," she said.

In another half an hour we were on Highway One, headed down the coast. It was one of those clear days where you could see for miles out across the Pacific Ocean, to the line where the water met the sky. All over the ocean were small whitecaps, blown up by a wind.

I made myself stay right here, in the car, next to my mother, instead of flying out across the water and imagining myself over *there*. Mom was quiet, her hands lightly turning the steering wheel as we snaked around the curves of the cliffs.

I kept sneaking glances at her. I wanted to tell her about the box, let her know the ghosts were after me as well as Dad. I wanted to tell her I'd let them out but I had no idea how to get them back in. I wanted to lean my head on her shoulder, and have her brush my hair back from my face and tell me everything would be okay.

"Penny for your thoughts," she said.

"They're worth a nickel," I said automatically. It was an old game we used to play when I was little. I'd stand near her, waiting, till she noticed me and then I'd tell her whatever was wrong: a girl teased me on the playground, or I had a headache, or I needed help with a book report. But this wasn't anything she could fix. Suddenly anger slammed down around the longing.

I shrugged and looked out the window. "Nothing," I said.

"Nothing?" she said.

"Nothing, nothing, nothing," I said to the white-caps and the dark blue line of the horizon.

We turned onto Russian River Road and headed east, then south on 101. After a few minutes we came to the exit for Santa Rosa, but instead of turning off, Mom drove right past it.

"Where're we going?" I asked.

"To the city."

"Really?" Mom and Dad never went all the way to San Francisco. "Do you know how to get there?" I asked.

Mom laughed, breaking the tension that had hovered between us. "Your dad and I used to live there," she said.

This was news to me. They often talked about how glad they were to live up the coast, in a little town, instead of in the crowded, busy Bay Area.

"When?" I asked.

"Before you," she said. "We met when I was going to college and your dad was living in the city. He worked in a gas station, and wrote poems at night. I met him at a poetry reading at a bookstore."

Dad? A poet?

I wasn't sure what to say to keep my mom talking.

But I didn't have to ask, she just kept going.

"He said he was like a cowboy poet—you know, those cowboys who write poetry while they are alone out there on the range with a bunch of cattle—but he said he was a gas pump poet, writing poetry in his mind while he pumped gas for people."

I still couldn't believe it. Poetry. My dad wrote poetry.

"Did you like his poems?"

"Very much," said Mom. "I was an English lit major, and all these profs gave boring lectures about the value of Brontë and Dante and here was a guy who wore blue jeans and wrote poems about everyday life."

I hadn't seen any of Dad's poems anywhere, even after going through every inch of the house. In fact, I'd never seen my dad write anything more than a lumber list.

"Does he still write poems?" I asked.

"No," she said. "He hasn't for a long time."

Mom somehow managed to snake through all the traffic in the city. We parked in a huge parking garage and walked for blocks to a bookstore called City Lights. The bookshelves were crammed together and the walls had doorways into other rooms full of books. Some of the floor was wood, some was linoleum. All of it was dirty. High on the walls were huge blown-up photographs of people—all authors, my mom said, taken when they gave readings at the store. Mom looked through shelves of poetry books, finally picking two, then moved over to another section. She had bright pink spots on her cheeks, like a kid hunting for Easter eggs.

I was bored. I looked at every picture on the walls.

So many of them were hippies, with long hair. One guy was wearing something that looked like a bathrobe, but with embroidery on it. I was surprised my mother lingered, looking at book after book. She usually said this kind of place made her fingers itch to clean up.

I stood by the window and watched all kinds of people hurry by on the crowded sidewalk. An old Chinese woman in a dark blue shirt and pants walked by, packages hanging from looped strings in both her hands. She was so old her hair was pure white and she leaned forward, as if her short, quick steps were all that kept her from falling on her face. Something about her opened up that scooped-out place in me. I wanted to run outside, call her back, wrap my arms around her, feel her arms wrapped around me.

I turned away, fast, from the window, hot tears burning under my eyelids.

Vietnam, Spring 1975

The heavy clouds made the night pitch-black. The village was quiet. I sat on the bed and waited, waited, waited. Had Grandmother been stopped by the soldiers again? Was she lying in her canoe, bruised and hurt, with no one to bring her hot tea? No one to row her back home?

Quan Am, I prayed, bring Grandmother safely back home. But only the ghosts, whispering and shuffling on the paths outside, answered me.

Suddenly the rain came, fast and hard, and something in me broke open with the clouds. I pulled open the bottom drawer of the bureau and grabbed the can of evaporated milk Má had brought. I squatted on the floor, put the tip of a knife to the top of the can, held it straight, and hit the handle with my fist. The tip of the knife bounced off the can. I put it back, hit it harder, and felt it slip in. I twisted the knife to open the hole, and pulled the knife back out.

I sucked out every drop of the rich, thick milk and crept back to the bed and listened to the rain rattling down on the palm fronds and dropping in bucketfuls to the ground outside.

"There you are," called my mom from the end of a row of books. She was holding a brown bag with books in it. "I'm ready." She swung open the door with her shoulder.

"Why do you like that bookstore so much?" I asked her as we made our way down the sidewalk.

She was quiet for a minute as we jostled through the crowd. I thought maybe she wasn't going to answer. "It reminds me of something," she said finally.

"Of what?"

"Oh . . . what was, maybe," she said, She waved her hand in front of her face like she was chasing away thoughts.

I'd never thought of my mom missing what used to be. I guess I never really thought of any time in her life before me and Dad. What was it she'd had that *she'd* lost?

"Your surprise next," Mom said. She grabbed me by the elbow, weaving us in and out of people. "I know it's still early, but we're going to get you some nice back-to-school clothes." She swept me into her excitement. I forgot all about what she was missing.

I didn't think they would have back-to-school clothes in the store so early in the summer, but we found some. Mom bought me two blouses, a heavy cotton skirt in a lavender and blue plaid, and a soft blue sweater. She gave a little gasp when the clerk rang up the total, but then turned and grinned at me. "Thanks to Redwood Cove Market," she said, and wrote out a check.

"You know," she said as she handed me the bag, "there's one more thing we should get here, then we'll go for lunch."

I followed her through the aisles and then we were suddenly at the counter in the lingerie department. My mother leaned across to the saleslady. She was stick-thin, dressed all in black, with a yellow tape measure draped around her neck. "My daughter needs a bra," she said.

"Mom, no!" I couldn't believe what she was saying.

"I understand," said the saleslady to me, her eyes flitting to my chest. "It can be a little embarrassing the first time for some girls."

"I don't need one," I said. "Let's go, Mom." I pulled on her arm and was instantly more embarrassed to be acting like a little kid.

The saleslady pulled the tape measure off her shoulders. "If you'll just step into the fitting room with me I'll see what size you need."

"I'm not going in there with you," I said, and crossed my arms over my chest. I felt like Gretel about to be shoved in the oven by the witch.

"Your mother can come in too, if you'd like."

Even worse.

The saleslady turned to my mom. "I tell you what. I've been doing this for more than twenty years. I can see your . . . did you say daughter?" She didn't wait for an answer. "Definitely a size twenty-eight, double A cup, to give a little growing room, you know," she said.

She walked over to a rack, rifled through, and pulled out two white bras. "One of these should be perfect," she said, and handed them to my mother.

"We'll take them both," Mom said. "Okay, Tracy?"

I nodded yes, that was fine, yes. I wandered back

into the aisle and stared at the mannequins while Mom paid. I hadn't said a word to anyone, but I'd been wondering when I would need a bra. I sure didn't want to ask my mom, and since I wasn't really friends with any of the girls in my class, I didn't know who to ask. It turned out a witchy saleslady had the answers.

৵

Mom navigated the sidewalks again and took me for lunch at a place called the Copper Kettle.

"You like your new clothes?" she asked, once we'd been seated. "Including the you-know-whats?"

"Mom," I said. "You should have warned me."

"I can see that," said Mom. "Actually, I didn't think of it till we were there."

She flipped open her menu. "I'm sorry, honey," she said. "I've never done this before."

And as fast as I'd gotten mad, I wasn't anymore.

"Me neither," I said.

"Like Grandee always says . . ."

"I know, I know!" I said. " 'Never do anything for the first time.' "

Mom looked around the restaurant. "Shopping for school clothes was a big deal for my mother," she said. "We'd go to the best stores, then have lunch, just like this. I see why she liked it so much." She smiled at me, then wrinkled her nose. "But we always bought the kind of clothes she liked, not me. Pink matching sweater sets, stuff like that."

"Is that why we never came to the city to go shopping before?"

She tipped her head to one side and looked carefully at me. "Probably those pink matching sweaters are the reason I did a lot of things."

"Like what?"

"Like . . ." She reached across the table and tapped me lightly on the nose. "Like you'll understand when you're older," she said.

I snatched her hand away. I wanted to say, "Mom, I understand more than you think." Grandee was always trying to make people into who she wanted them to be. Even from three thousand miles away, she was always telling Mom what to do.

Mom shook her head slightly. Maybe she was thinking about the same thing.

I ordered a hamburger, and Mom had French onion soup. She kept reaching into the bread basket and tearing off another hunk of the crusty white bread and slathering it with butter. I took one bite and nearly spit it out. It tasted sour, kind of vinegary.

Mom laughed. "It's called sourdough bread," she said. "San Francisco's famous for it." After we finished she begged an extra basket of bread from the busboy. She slid the bread onto her lap and wrapped it in her cloth napkin. "For Dad," she whispered. "Sourdough, a chunk of cheese, and a bottle of Italian red wine in Washington Square Park. That was a big date for us—no money."

Usually, not having enough money was something my parents fought about. But now she made it sound so . . . romantic. I tried to imagine my parents sitting outside on a blanket, my dad reading his poetry to my mom. It was disturbing to think they had a time I knew nothing about. A time when they laughed and drank red wine together.

Mom snuck the bread and napkin into my bag.

"Don't worry," she whispered, and winked at me. "I didn't take the butter. Your clothes are safe."

It wasn't my clothes I was worried about. It was her. Stealing bread and napkins. I didn't even know she knew how to wink.

Vietnam, Spring 1975

I woke in the dark, the rain still pouring off the edge of the roof. I had slid sideways down the wall and was curled up in a ball. Stomach cramps ran through me. I needed to get to the outhouse, fast.

I ran through the rain to the choppy river and over the monkey bridge. Three, four, five steps and I was squatting inside, one thin plank under each foot. The air was cold and wet against my bare skin.

Quan Am, Quan Am, I prayed, don't let ma nuoc, the water ghost, find me. Don't let it grab me, its sharp teeth biting, chewing, working its way inside.

Once I'd asked Grandmother what the water ghost looked like. "Who knows?" she'd said. "You never know it's after you until it's too late."

Dinner was easy. Mom had insisted we buy fresh raviolis in North Beach before we left. Dad even leaned over and kissed Mom in the middle of dinner.

"You remembered," he said.

"Um-hum," she said.

"Remembered what?" I asked. Here it was again, between them in the kitchen, the time before me. "What?" I said again.

"I proposed to your mom one night in a little restaurant in North Beach," he said. "After raviolis," he said, "and before spumoni ice cream."

"Holding hands next to that candle stuck in an old Chianti bottle, with the wax dripping all kinds of colors." Mom's face was soft, her eyes full of tears, the good kind of tears.

"Lucky you didn't bring home any spumoni ice cream," Dad said.

"Why not?" I asked.

"Tastes terrible," he said.

"I thought you liked it!" Mom said.

He shook his head. "Nope. Only ate it to impress you."

"I was more impressed by your . . ."

Dad laughed out loud and tipped his chair back

onto two legs. The chair balanced perfectly, and every muscle in his body relaxed. "Go on," he said, "impressed by my what?"

"Bob," she said, and blushed bright red, but she was laughing herself.

"You know what I mean!" she said. "Your—"

He interrupted her again. "My kisses, sweeter than wine?"

"Oh, hush," she said, and gave him a light tap on the chest.

By then I was blushing myself, like I was watching something private I wasn't supposed to see.

Mom jumped up. "I'll show you what impressed me." She pulled two books out of the bag sitting on the counter and put them down next to his plate.

He picked them up slowly, slid them apart, and stared at the covers.

"I . . . I thought you might find them inspiring," she said, and sat down, like all the strength had drained out of her legs. "Maybe write a little poetry again . . ." She faltered.

He stood up stiffly, like a jointed wooden doll. "Thank you," he said with effort. He put the books back down and left the room.

Mom stared at the books. "I think that means no," she whispered.

৵

A click outside woke me up. It was the sound of Dad's truck door opening, quietly. Was someone breaking into his truck? I slid out of bed and crossed to the window, then heard a louder click of metal on metal as someone closed the car door. When I opened the curtains a crack I could see the dark outline of a man sitting in the truck, his hands on the steering wheel. Then he leaned sideways, and the light from the glove compartment shone on his face.

It was my dad, his eyes dark circles in the light. He peered into the glove compartment, rummaged through it, raised his hand. The dogtag swung at the end of the chain. The light suddenly snapped off. I blinked twice and my eyes adjusted to the darkness again. He was sitting stiffly upright, hands rigid on the steering wheel. His shoulders began to shake, then he slumped forward until his forehead rested on the steering wheel, his shoulders heaving.

I was a mess of feelings. Partly I was excited—now I knew where the dogtag was. Partly I was frightened to see—or almost see—my dad cry. I was used to him being angry, and beat-up looking, but I'd never seen him look so broken apart. I was suddenly ashamed to be spying on him and dropped the curtain and crept back to my bed.

It wasn't long until my dad came back in the front door. In the stillness, the quiet rooms of our house echoed with secrets.

I waited a long, long time, then waited some more. When I was absolutely sure Dad was asleep, I slipped out the back door. I wasn't going to let the dogtag disappear again.

Vietnam, Spring 1975

I woke again. The rain had stopped. I could smell the mist rolling off the river. I stretched out, warm, unafraid, even in the dark. It was as if my fear had left with the pounding rain. I imagined Grandmother sleeping in the canoe under the shelter of a bridge, dry, safe. She must have been delayed by the rain. Surely tomorrow she would be home.

There was a scratching sound near the back, soft footfalls in the kitchen. Breathing. In one move I was crouching on the bed. I could fly out the front door, run down the path. But what if there were worse dangers outside? Had the fighting come to the village?

I slid under the bed.

"Amazing," Stargazer kept saying. "Look at this Viking helmet," he said, waving one of the pictures from the class bulletin board at me. We were sitting next to each other on the top stair of the trailer.

"All that metal really would stop just about anything," he said. "Do you think we could make a helmet like that?"

"I think it would be easier to make shields. At least they're sort of flat."

"True," said Stargazer.

Summer wandered out of the trailer and tried to climb into Stargazer's lap.

Stargazer put his elbows out, blocking her. She tried a couple times to get past his arms, then snuggled into my arms and watched him study the picture.

"What're you doing in there?" I asked her.

"Washing potatoes with Beldon," she said. "Looking for bunnies."

Summer leaned back against me, and under my shirt, the dogtag scraped lightly against my house key.

"What's that?" she said, and patted my T-shirt.

"Just my key," I said.

"Lemme see," she said, and pulled at the neck of my shirt.

"Cut it out!" I said, grabbing her hands. "You can't go reaching into people's shirts, Summer."

She looked at me in surprise. "Why not?"

"It's private inside your shirt. Especially for girls." *Especially for me, right that minute,* I thought. I'd put on one of the bras Mom had bought me. It felt a little tight around my chest, but mostly good, and soft. But the last person I wanted to know I was wearing a bra was Stargazer.

"I'm a girl," Summer said. "You can look inside my shirt." She pulled her shirt up to show me her stomach. "See?"

I almost said, "You'll understand when you're older," but for one thing, I would have sounded just like my mother, and for another thing, she might have asked me what I meant and I didn't want the conversation to go anywhere near there with Stargazer around. Instead I put my face right next to her ear and whispered, "Tummy-gummy." In a flash she was off my lap and at the bottom of the stairs, daring me to come after her.

Summer was fast, but so was I. I caught up with her under a buckeye tree next to the garden and we tumbled to the ground in the dry grass. I grabbed her in a one-armed bear hug and tried to get to her stomach while she shrieked and giggled. I finally gave up and lay back in the grass, panting and laughing.

A shadow fell across my face, blocking out the sun. It was Stargazer, holding out a page to me. "We could make shields like this," he said, then stopped and dropped to his knees beside me, staring at my shirt. "Cool," he whispered.

I felt for the chain, slid my hand down. There were the dogtag and key, lying right on my shirt.

Summer sat up and stared at my shirt. Her eyes widened in surprise and she grabbed for the chain.

"Me," said Summer, "me first." She threw herself on top of me, tugging on the chain. I twisted out from under her and jumped to my feet.

"Leave me alone!" I shouted. "Both of you. Just leave me alone." I couldn't believe that the dogtag—so mysterious and full of secrets—was just a toy they were fighting over.

I reached for the dogtag to put it back under my shirt, but the chain wasn't around my neck anymore.

Stargazer and Summer scrabbled in the grass by my feet. Stargazer shot up, holding the chain over his head. The dogtag and key twisted and turned at the end of the chain. Summer leaped up and banged her fists against Stargazer. "Lemme see, lemme see," she howled.

"No," he said. "I got it."

"Mine," Summer yelled.

"Give it back," I said, reaching for it, but Stargazer twisted away from both of us.

"What's going on out there?" Beldon called from the porch.

Stargazer didn't answer. Summer grabbed his shirt and tried to climb up his legs. "Meeee!" she howled. "No fair!"

"Ow, you just hit me in the neck, Summer!" Stargazer yelled.

Beldon thudded down the stairs, and then he was beside us.

"Quit teasing her, Stargazer," he said. He grabbed the chain and held it out for Summer. Suddenly his face turned white and he pulled his hand back and stared at the dogtag.

"Where'd you get this?" he said to Stargazer. His voice was deadly quiet.

"It's Tracy's," Stargazer said, and took a step back.

Beldon turned on me.

"This your father's?" he said, but it was more a statement than a question.

I stared at him. No, it wasn't. Yes, it was. I didn't answer.

Beldon closed his fist around the dogtag. "Baby killer," he said. He spat the words out like swear words. Summer and Stargazer stood perfectly still, as if any movement might make them some kind of target.

Beldon held his fist up to my face. "He lets you carry this around to brag about his brave, glory days in the army? That man is twisted."

He spun away, threw the chain and metal as far as he could toward the river, then turned back to me. "We're about peace here, not about killing, you understand?"

Vietnam, Spring 1975

Light footsteps came into the room, right to the bed, as if someone knew I was there, my heart hammering so hard it must be shaking the bed from where I hid underneath. I pressed harder against the back wall, breathed slow and tight. Someone knelt beside the bed, knees nearly touching me. I could hear hands sliding over the reed mat, patting, feeling. "Where are you?" he whispered. "A ghost doesn't leave a warm quilt."

I said nothing.

"Tell me, why are you afraid of your own son?"

Could it be one of my uncles?

I opened my mouth to speak, but nothing came out.

I tried again. "Grandmother is . . ."

There was a scuttling on the floor as he moved away, then a thump as he dropped to the ground.

Silence.

I heard him catch his breath on the other side of the room. "I'm third son," he said. "I've been away in the north, for one year."

"Uncle Luc?" I said softly, but I didn't move from under the bed.

"Who are you?" he replied. I was afraid to answer. How did I know he was really Uncle Luc?

I waited.

"I've had no news of my family for a long time," he said. "When I left, my brother was in the army, one sister in Saigon, one working in the laundry at the American base."

"My mother," I said.

He grunted. "Is she still alive?"

I slid out from under the bed, but sat close enough to go back under fast. "Má came for the autumn festival," I said. "Sometimes she brings money. American dollars." Everyone knew the power of American dollars, passed hand to hand in the marketplace to buy fruit and vegetables, charcoal, pork, and chicken.

In the silence I thought, "He must hate my mother for working with the enemy."

"She's very brave," I whispered. "She steals bandages and alcohol and American medicines."

"I can't stay long," he said. "Quickly, give me news of the family."

I told him what I knew as dawn edged into the room and I could see his gray shape, sitting against the far wall. When I told him that Grandmother had not come home, he sucked his breath in through his teeth. It must have scared him too.

"Maybe I can go with you?" I asked.

"No. Stay hidden. The fighting will be here very soon." He rose to his feet and I jumped to mine.

He put his hand on top of my head. "You've grown while I've been gone," he said. He reached into his pocket and pulled out a small photo and set it carefully on the altar on top of the bureau.

"For Grandmother," he said. "And in case you're the only one left . . ." He stopped, and I heard him swallow.

"Shhh," I said. I didn't want him to say anything more.

I wondered if Stargazer would show up the next morning. He would, if he wasn't forbidden to come over.

I didn't have to wait long. My parents both left early in the morning—Mom was stocking shelves and had to be in at six, and Dad left at 7:20. A few minutes later Stargazer knocked on my window. I saw his shadow as he cupped his hands around his face and pressed up against the window.

"Tracy."

I lay perfectly still.

"It's me, Stargazer."

Obviously.

"I'm sorry about Beldon," he said. The glass blurred his voice. "You know, about what he said." The shadow shifted as he pressed his ear to the glass, then his face again.

"I know you're in there."

My dad did not kill babies.

"C'mon, Tracy."

He was a *soldier*, doing his job.

"And I know you're listening to me."

Soldiers fight other soldiers. They don't go around killing babies.

Or women. Or children.

"I have it." There was an impatient *click-click-click* of metal against glass.

War has rules.

"I got the dogtag back for you."

༈

When I opened the back door he was standing there, waiting for me, holding the dogtag on the end of the open chain.

"Where'd you find it?" I asked.

"Under a huckleberry bush," he said. "But the chain's broken. And I didn't find your key. Different weights, you know. The key must have gone farther when Beldon . . ." He trailed off.

He put it in my hand. "It's not your dad's," he said. The tiny metal beads of the chain were cool in my palm. Right in the middle, two of them were no longer connected.

"I know."

"So who's James Kirby? Is he a friend of your dad's? Why was his dogtag in your dad's ammo box?"

I shook my head, stared at the dogtag. A thin line of dark dirt was still crusted around the edge. When I'd snuck it out of the glove compartment two nights ago I'd held it in my cupped hands, tight to my nose, and thought I smelled the tang of metal and dirt and sweat. I wasn't about to smell it now, in front of Stargazer, but I rubbed my thumb over it, felt the tiny bumps of the letters stamped into the metal.

KIRBY, JAMES B.
973-00-8847
TYPE O POS
NO PREF

I had no idea why my dad had James B. Kirby's dog-tag. All I had were a bunch of unanswered questions piled up, one on top of the other. Ammo box and dog-tag, "you, me, and Bluto," my dad leaning over his steering wheel, shoulders heaving.

"Maybe it's Bluto's," Stargazer said.

"What?" I said.

"Like Bluto is a nickname for James. Get it? Maybe your dad kept it when they all came home, 'cause Bluto was a hero, and he thought maybe it would rub off on him."

Stargazer's eyes were shining. His ideas about war and heroes and guns were so stupid. How had we ever become friends? He had no idea at all who I was, the part of me I'd left *there*, the hungry ghosts that circled around, coming closer and closer, pressing in on me.

Suddenly, like an explosion of dirt and rocks after a bomb hits, anger erupted out of me. My fist shot out and smashed into Stargazer's face. He fell over back-ward onto the porch, then staggered up to his feet.

"What're you doing?" he said. He didn't look mad, just surprised. He put his hand up to his face.

"Go away!" I yelled, even though he was only a few feet away. "My dad"—I shoved him in the chest—"is not a baby killer." I shoved him again.

Now Stargazer was starting to look mad.

"I didn't say he was. Beldon did." He tried to grab my wrists, but I knocked his hands away. "He didn't mean it."

"Yes he did." I looked at Stargazer and realized I wanted to hit him again, and that it would feel good. The feeling scared me. "Get out of here!" I said. I could feel my teeth clenching so tight my jaw hurt.

"Fine," said Stargazer, backing down the porch stairs. "I'm going. What's wrong with you, anyway?"

I followed him down the driveway as he pulled his bike away from the wall by my bedroom window. I thought for one second, *He's running again, only this time from me, not my dad. Good*, I thought, *good.*

His bike wobbled as he pedaled down the driveway. At the sidewalk he put his foot down, turned around and yelled, "Beldon says your mother was a prostitute.

Lots of them had GI babies. Like you." Then he took off.

I ran to the sidewalk and screamed after him, "I hate your guts! And your stupid father's too!"

I sat on the back porch and didn't move.

Stargazer was gone.

There was gone.

I was cut off from everyone, everything.

The ghosts had won. They'd eaten me away from the inside.

Vietnam, Spring 1975

I took the photo from Quan Am's altar and walked outside so I could see it better. Uncle Luc, in his North Vietnamese Army uniform. How could he be so brave, standing with his shoulders back, a proud, calm look in his eyes?

I thought about what he didn't say: in case he was killed in the big fight coming up, we could take care of his spirit at the altar, so he wouldn't be a hungry ghost with no one to set food out for him, or burn paper clothes and money for him.

I slid the photo into my pocket.

When the big American planes flew overhead during the day, I took out Uncle Luc's picture, and stared at his calm eyes. If he could be brave, so could I.

I slipped the dogtag into my pocket and kept my hand around it in a tight fist. Then I headed for the beach, taking the path beside the Redwood Cove Market and dropping down onto the sand. I didn't walk out into the water to feel the waves rush up against my legs and pull back out. I wasn't quite sure if I would see the big sucker waves coming toward me in time to head back up the beach. I wasn't sure if I would care if I noticed them in time. That should have scared me as much as wanting to hurt Stargazer, but it didn't.

I stared out at the water, watched a fishing boat motor north toward the Seal Point Pier to unload its catch. Dozens of seagulls dipped and soared in big circles around the boat, their raucous calls coming all the way to the beach.

I figured Beldon was right. Probably my mother was a prostitute. There were always women who slept with soldiers, no matter where the war was. I bet they had to, just to survive. And sometimes they had babies. That was also just the way things were. But they probably couldn't raise those babies. I bet they cried and cried when they gave them to somebody else to raise. Somebody old. Somebody who loved them even if their mother was a prostitute. Even if they had round eyes and light hair.

I found a little protected spot at the base of the cliffs where I could lie down and let the hot sun soak into my back and let the sound of the waves lull me to sleep.

❧

I woke up to a cold, wet fog lying over the beach. The sun was a bright red smudge heading toward the fog-shrouded ocean. It must be late afternoon. I was lying in the exact same position, with my hands one on top of the other, underneath my cheek. I stood up and shook the pins and needles out of my arms and headed home.

As I walked up the hill, I decided I wouldn't tell anyone. Not about the fight with Stargazer, not the obvious truth about my blood mother being a prostitute. I made my face so none of my feelings showed. My hidden face was my only protection from my dad's shaking hands and the ice clicking in his bourbon glass as the ghosts—our ghosts—circled.

I suddenly wondered: how much did my parents know? They must have known about my blood mother.

Then I thought: *what if they didn't know?* Would they send me away—like I was somehow tainted? Or would my mother brush it all aside. "We wanted a daughter, and you needed a home," as if that was the answer to everything. Thoughts were flying through my mind like the seagulls circling the fishing boat, noisy and unsettled.

Mom's car was in front of our house when I got back. Of course. When she went to work early, she was home early. I paused at the front door, reached up for my key chain, felt my bare neck.

I suddenly felt too tired to even walk around and see if the back door was unlocked. I knocked and Mom answered the door, looked at me in surprise. "Where's your key?" she said.

I stepped inside, glad for the dusky light in the entry hall. "I lost it." I was surprised how normal my voice sounded. "Swimming in the creek with Stargazer. My hand caught in the chain and broke it. We couldn't find it."

Mom crossed her arms. "I don't like you swimming in water that deep, Tracy."

"It's okay. Ruthie was with us."

"Is she a strong swimmer?"

"Mom. Can you quit with the twenty questions?" I slipped past her and headed for my room.

I sat down on my bed and pulled the dogtag out of my pocket. I knew I should put it back in the truck. I promised myself that I would. Soon. But my ex-friend Stargazer had given me an idea.

᠁

At dinner that night Mom got going again on my swimming with Stargazer.

"I just don't like it," she said. "Ruthie may be a strong swimmer, but she's going to have a baby at any time now."

Dad looked at me and gave a tiny shrug. We were both used to Mom and her worries. "Where do you swim in the river?" he asked.

"You know, Dad, if you walk upstream from Stargazer's trailer for about ten or fifteen minutes. There's a bend in the river and nice flat rocks on the bank to dry out on."

"I know that spot," said Dad. "I've caught a few big fish there where the river widens out and undercuts the bank as it turns."

"That's it," I said. "We try to catch crayfish there. They're all sitting under that bank wiggling their feelers, trying to catch something coming downstream."

Dad turned back to Mom. "The current's really slow there," he said. "I'm sure Ruthie could get them out of any trouble they got in."

Mom sighed. "All right," she said. "Just promise me you won't go swimming alone with Stargazer there this summer."

That was an easy promise to make. I didn't plan on doing anything with Stargazer this summer.

⌒

As soon as my parents left the next morning I jumped out of bed and dressed. I pulled the photo out of my dad's drawer, but finding a magnifying glass took forever. I knew I'd seen one somewhere, a while ago, but I just couldn't remember where. Finally I found it in a crowded kitchen drawer, between the vegetable peeler and the ice cream scoop.

I took the photo and magnifying glass out to the porch. I could see the thin line of the chain on all three GIs' necks, and on the muscular one, the one we figured was Bluto, the tag lay on top of his T-shirt.

I looked through the magnifying glass. I could see there were tiny bumps from the letters, but I couldn't read them. I put the magnifying glass back in the drawer.

"You, me, and Bluto."

Who was "Bluto"? Who was "me"? Who was James B. Kirby, and why did his dogtag make my dad cry?

༄

That night I asked about Bluto, blurting out the question without thinking. One minute I was winding spaghetti around my fork, the next minute two little words jumped out of my mouth.

Dad looked shocked. He set down his fork. "What?" he said.

"Who's Bluto?" I repeated.

Mom looked from one to the other of us, cleared her throat like she was going to say something.

"Bluto was a buddy of mine in Nam," Dad said.

Mom gave a little gasp. Dad glanced at her, then looked back at me.

"Vietnam. We called it *Nam* for short," he said.

Nam. It was like a thin glass bubble around the word had shattered. *Nam* hung in the air between the three of us.

"What happened to him?"

"Last I heard, he was headed back home to Indiana."

I didn't even want to breathe, didn't want to disturb anything.

"So he's still alive?"

I could feel Dad tensing, pulling back. "How do you know about Bluto?"

"I saw a picture of him. In your sock drawer."

"What were you doing snooping in his drawer?" Mom said.

"I wasn't," I said, trying to sound unjustly accused. "I found it when I was putting away the laundry."

"Uh-huh." Dad didn't sound like he believed me.

Mom put up her hand. "I don't see why . . . This all happened so long ago."

"Is Bluto his real name?" I asked softly, not wanting Dad to run.

"Drop it, Tracy," Mom said. She looked nervously from me to Dad.

I couldn't. Not now. Not when I was so close to getting some information.

"His name was Gifford L. Hairston the Third," Dad said. "Sometimes we called him Sticks for the 'Third' part. He was a big guy, with an even bigger name."

Mom smiled a tight, thin smile. "I didn't know that."

"You never asked," said Dad. He stood up, grabbed his plate.

"Who's the other guy? The skinny one?"

Dad's face slammed shut. "A buddy," he said. His plate clattered into the sink. "A good buddy."

"What was his name?" I asked. My voice sounded high and squeaky. Please, Dad, please tell me.

"Rooster," said Dad as he left the room. "We called him Rooster."

Vietnam, Spring 1975

The village was silent. No cooking fires were lit, no one traveled on the paths, boats were tied up. Fighting was coming.

I stood on the porch and looked up the river. The sun had almost set behind the trees. Hidden in the reeds, the shore birds called mournfully to one another, Too-et, too-et.

Even looking at Uncle Luc's photo didn't help anymore. Fear roared up in me, telling me I was alone, alone. Grandmother was never going to come back. I was as alone as a wandering ghost.

Without thinking, I pushed off the porch and onto the path. The dirt was still soft from the rain. Step after step I ran, stretching out my legs, the evening air burning in my chest, pushing deep into the emptiness and fear in my belly.

When I couldn't take one more breath I slowed down

and walked, then trotted like the women who carry two baskets balanced on the ends of a bamboo pole. When I could, I ran hard again, my breath loud in my ears. The path widened, big enough for a water buffalo, big enough for three bicycles, big enough for a car. I ran toward Da Nang, toward Má, ran to be alive and not a ghost.

For the next couple of days I stayed in my room and read. I read all of the Laura Ingalls Wilder books. I even read every *Sunset* (Mom's) and *Time* (Dad's) magazine Mom had stacked in tidy piles.

The third day the phone rang. I lay on my bed and counted seven rings before the person hung up. A few minutes later it started again. Seven more rings.

It had to be Stargazer. At first, my heart pounded so hard it made me dizzy. And if I picked up the phone would he be on the other end, or would there just be silence, emptiness? He called twice more, then quit.

I kept reading. I read to keep my mind full of other people's words, I read so I wouldn't hear my own thoughts, I read to shut out the howls of the ghosts. I read so I wouldn't feel erased, swept away by the winds blowing high overhead between *there* and here.

I kept the broken chain and the dogtag under my

mattress. When I read I pulled out the dogtag. I pretended it was nighttime and Dad was reading to me, weaving me into his life, word by word. While I read, I rubbed the dogtag against my cheek, slid it down my neck to the tiny scar right above my collarbone, then back up to my cheek again.

"Good night, Rooster."

"Good night, chickadee."

Bluto = Gifford L. Hairston the Third.

Did Rooster = James B. Kirby?

⌇

Mom left her door key and a dollar on the kitchen counter for me to get a new key made. Every night she asked me why I hadn't gotten the key copied. Finally I took a dollar out of my underwear drawer, grabbed mom's money and key off the counter, and rode my bike over to Jones Brothers.

One of the hardware guys copied my key, and I picked out a twenty-four-inch bead chain necklace from the punchboard wall where all the key chains hung. I strung my new key on it, slipped it over my head, then took my money up to Mr. Conner.

"Stargazer's been here a couple of times," Mr. Conner

said as I handed him my two dollars. "He was buying wallpaper paste to make papier-mâché."

I didn't say anything.

"Came back yesterday, said the paste wasn't strong enough, and bought some white glue."

"So what?" I said.

"Oh," he said. "So that's the way it is." The cash register drawer slid open. Mr. Conner put the money in and counted out the change slowly, like he was thinking.

He dropped the coins into my hand. "He looks lonely, Monkey."

As if Mr. Conner had any idea what had happened between me and Stargazer, like it was somehow my fault. "Don't call me Monkey," I said. "I hate it."

Mr. Conner took a step back, his eyebrows flying up in surprise.

"I didn't know," he said softly. "Got it, Tracy."

I stuffed the change in my pocket and left, with a bad feeling that I had somehow lost something.

Vietnam, Spring 1975

Right here by the river, with the sliver of moon in the sky, this is where the American jeep with the bright lights and stink of gasoline caught me, my hands in fists, my mouth empty of words. Jeep doors slammed, a hand grabbed my shoulder, and I smelled the pig smell of an American who eats too much meat.

Rough voices argued over my fate, one American, one Vietnamese. He asked: where are you running?

"To my mother, who works on the base in the laundry room." Now they would take me to Má so I didn't have to run any farther.

The man talked with the pig-smell man. He nodded, said things I didn't understand, held tight to my shoulder. They argued back and forth. It looked like the American wanted to leave me and go, wasn't going to take me to Má.

He noticed my hand, holding tight to something; I didn't know what. He opened my fingers, pulled out a small piece of paper, and held it up to the headlights. He gave a low, American whistle, and passed it to the other man.

In the flash of the headlights, I saw. It was Uncle Luc, in his uniform.

I bit into the American's hand holding tight to my shoulder. It tasted of salt and metal. He lifted his hand to his mouth and I jumped in the tall grass by the side of the road. I fell to my knees and crawled, fast, toward the muddy ditch.

A boot came down on my leg. The pig-smell American grabbed me and threw me into the back of the jeep.

When I wheeled my bike into the backyard I noticed two pieces of paper, folded and refolded, and stuck between the boards in the fence.

I pulled out the smaller one and unfolded it. There were two lines, in Stargazer's cramped writing:

Diabrotica (in the garden).

Great blue heron (in the river). It flew away when it saw me.

I pulled out the second note.

Please call me. Please, he wrote again, then under-lined it three times.

I was hit with a longing so sharp it hurt. It was miss-ing Stargazer, and more. It was Summer and Ruthie and the baby I would probably never see. It was trying to catch crayfish in the river, and sizzling on the hot rocks. It was my future and my American past, all rolled into one.

I could call him. We could go on being friends after he mumbled "Sorry" and I said "It's okay." I imag-ined dialing his number, waiting for him to pick up the phone, imagined hearing Summer in the background while we talked.

Then I looked at that underlined *please*, as if saying *please* like a prompted three-year-old could be enough, and my heart slammed shut again. I wadded up the papers and threw them in the garbage can.

Then I pulled one out, went into the kitchen, and grabbed a pencil.

Quit leaving notes, I wrote, and jammed it into the fence.

Tension kept building up at my house, like a bottle of soda that somebody won't leave off shaking. Dad was quiet at dinner, staring at his plate and answering in grunts when Mom asked him questions. He couldn't keep his hands from shaking, and started wrapping both hands around his glass to lift it off the table.

༈

Stargazer didn't stop leaving me notes. He must have come by really early every morning. First they were just the names of a few animals, and then he started to add details, like:

Barn owl. Teaching her babies to hunt at dusk. Summer says she doesn't want them to eat the bunnies.

Two ravens. Chased away from the garden by a group of tiny blackbirds.

༈

Seven mornings, seven notes. I laid them out on my bed and pulled my key chain over my head. I slid the chain from hand to hand, gathered the little stainless steel beads in one palm, then the other. Tonight, I promised myself. Tonight I'd sneak out to Dad's truck and put the dogtag back.

I pressed the back of the dogtag into the soft skin inside my forearm. I held it there, pushing hard with the heel of my hand. When I pulled it away, I could read the words on my arm.

I slipped the chain back over my head. Tomorrow. I'd put it back tomorrow.

The next day the note was fatter. I pulled it out and unfolded it. There were two sheets of paper.

The boat is ready. I let Summer use my watercolors to draw this. The full moon is the day after tomorrow. Please come at midnight. I'll be at the crayfish hole, like we planned.

I sat on the back porch and smoothed out Summer's drawing on my leg. I could make out the ship with its sails, and a row of shields on the side, painted in big, careful circles. Her brush was full of paint at the beginning of each circle, and thin and pale at the end. I bet she'd let Stargazer help her make those nice round circles. The sky looked like she'd used every color in the paint set. On the very edge was tiny writing by Stargazer. I turned the page sideways.

Summer says that blob on the front of the ship is a

Viking bunny. P.S. I just read this to her and she says it is not a blob, it is a BUNNY, just ask Jip and Pixie.

The drawing made me happy and sad at the same time.

Vietnam, Spring 1975

In the morning the Vietnamese man came and got me from the little room where I'd slept. I followed him down a long hall. He wore shoes like an American and planted his feet hard on the ground, instead of walking softly in sandals that would let the rain dry off and the heat get out.

He brought me to an American sitting at a desk who had a face shut up tight. Not like a man who is afraid and tries to hurt you first, but something worse.

The American and the Vietnamese talked and pointed at me and talked some more, and then the Vietnamese told me to sit on the bench by the American Boss Man's desk and he walked out of the room.

A few minutes later he came back, followed by a woman walking behind him with a soft shush-shush-shush of sandals. I stared hard at the floor. I wasn't sure I could make my face look like nothing if it was my mother. The American asked her questions in English, questions I didn't understand, but I could tell by her voice. It was Má.

She answered in a mix of Vietnamese and English and I understood enough: Yes, she had a daughter. Yes, the daughter's father was American, from here on the base. Her daughter was a good girl. She would never work with the North Vietnamese.

Then the Boss Man asked another question, but this time she didn't answer. The Vietnamese repeated: "The girl was carrying this picture when we picked her up. Who is it?"

"I don't know," she said, still using the voice all the villagers use when they are in danger. It is a voice that gives away nothing, from their face that shows nothing. But if you listen carefully there is always a trembling inside that voice.

"Honestly, what's with you two," Mom said that night at dinner. Dad glanced up at her. "Nothing," he said. I just shrugged.

"Somebody say something," Mom finally said. "What did you do all day, Tracy?"

"Read."

"I never thought I'd say it, but why aren't you spending more time with Stargazer?"

I shrugged again.

Mom looked at me in surprise but didn't say anything. For a long time there was just the sound of our forks scraping the plates, our glasses clicking when we put them back down on the table.

Mom banged down her fork and Dad and I both jumped. "I asked you a question, Bob," she said.

I hadn't heard it either.

"Sorry," he said, without even looking up. "What?"

"I said, my mother called. She wants us to come visit for Thanksgiving this fall."

Dad grunted and shoved a big piece of bread in his mouth.

"What do you think?"

"Why don't you go and take Tracy," he said.

"She invited us all. Let's do something together as a family for once," Mom said.

Dad shoved his chair back from the table. "I'm missing the news," he said, and left the room.

"Don't walk out on me!" Mom yelled after him. "We're in the middle of a conversation."

She turned on me. "What's going on around here? Ever since you looked in your baby book and started asking me questions, things have been tense. Weird, with both of you."

There was so much she didn't know. I opened my mouth, shut it again. I didn't have words for the empty, scooped-out place in me, didn't know how to talk about *there*.

Mom stared at me. "Well? What?"

I could tell the ghosts were howling around her now too, and I had no idea how to make them stop.

Dad suddenly reappeared and grabbed the back of his chair in both hands. His knuckles were white, he was holding on so tightly. "Okay, I won't watch the news," he said to Mom. "Let's talk. What would you like to talk about?"

Mom looked reckless, like she knew she should leave him alone, but she just couldn't. She took a deep breath. "While you were in Nam, I watched all three newscasts every night, one after the other. And I prayed those deaths—those men reduced to meaningless numbers that Cronkite read off every night—I prayed they were other people, not you. And I hated myself for wishing them dead, just because I didn't know them."

Mom rubbed her hand across her forehead.

"You didn't die, but you're not alive either," she said. "What happened?"

"Nam happened," Dad said in a flat voice, like that explained everything. His feelings, her feelings, everything wrapped tight in that one little word, *Nam*. He let go of the chair and brushed past her. "I'm going out. I might be a while."

He blinked at me, like he was surprised to see me, then headed out the back door, easing it shut behind him.

Vietnam, Spring 1975

The Vietnamese man walked over to me, pushed up my chin. "What kind of rude, con lai *daughter are you?*" he said. "Say hello to your mother."

He grabbed Má and yanked her in front of me.

"This is not my daughter," she said, from her face that showed nothing. "My daughter is very beautiful. You are mistaken."

"Perhaps it has been too long since you have seen her," he said. "Look carefully."

The American Boss Man grabbed me by the arm and twisted it behind my back. I heard a pop in my shoulder and then the room was red and black and I was screaming and I heard my mother wail.

"Stop," she said. "Please stop. Don't hurt her."

The Boss Man suddenly pinned me up against the wall

with one hand on my chest. My toes barely brushed the floor. He was talking and the Vietnamese was talking at the same time. "Who is in the photo your daughter was carrying?"

My mother was staring back and forth at me and the American, her eyes begging.

"You're a snake in our nest," said the Vietnamese to my mother.

The Boss Man pulled a knife from his belt. He put the tip of the blade up to my neck. Very slowly, he let me slide down onto the sharp tip. I felt a tiny sting in my neck, like the sting of a wasp.

"Má," I cried. I didn't mean to. Just one word, and then I couldn't stuff it back in my mouth.

"Too-et," cried Má. She rushed to me, tried to push me higher up the wall. "Stop," she cried. "Yes, she is my daughter." Her arms were shaking and shivering.

"And the photo?"

"My brother," said my mother, panting.

The Boss Man lowered his knife. He stepped back and I fell to the floor.

Light from the living room slanted in through my door. I could hear Mom turning the pages in a magazine, little papery slaps as she paged restlessly through, put down the magazine, flipped on the TV, then turned it off.

Dad still hadn't come home.

I tried to stay awake, but I must have been dozing, because I woke up, suddenly and completely, hearing Dad's truck pull into the driveway.

I jumped up and eased my door open a crack. Mom was sitting on the couch, rubbing her eyes. She must have been there all this time.

Dad came in and stood in front of her.

"Where've you been?" Mom asked.

"Slept in my truck." He looked like he had.

"You can't just say 'Nam happened' and walk out on us."

"Let's not fight. I have to work tomorrow."

"We don't have to fight, you just have to listen." Mom's voice was sharp, desperate. "Do you know what it was like for me, while you were in Nam? No, don't interrupt. Even now when the phone rings, I hate it. Every call from one of the other army wives, it always started the same—'It's okay, it's me, everything's all right.' Every knock on the door was a nightmare. I was sure it was someone coming to tell me you were dead.

"And you just say 'Nam happened' and walk out,

and I'm left at home, waiting. Vietnam's still happening, don't you see? I can't keep waiting, waiting for you to come back to me."

"Are you done?"

"Is that all you have to say? Am I done?"

There was a pause, then Dad spoke. "I wish I'd never gone." His voice was flat. "Is that what you want to hear me say?" He gave a harsh laugh. "But I don't recall the draft board asking for my opinion."

"What happened to you over there?" Mom said. "Just tell me something, anything, about how you felt over there."

Silence.

When Dad began speaking, his voice was so soft I could barely hear him.

"One night a couple months before I came home I was on guard duty. It was unbelievably still, quiet. I was so afraid."

More silence.

"Not of being killed, but because I couldn't remember your face, what your laugh sounded like, what it felt like to touch you. But in the morning I realized that when I saw you again, it would be all right."

The silence stretched out, filled with emptiness. I

realized I was holding my breath, and let it out as quietly as I could.

"But it's not all right, is it?"

"Oh, Bob," Mom whispered, then something I couldn't hear.

"I don't know either," Dad said. There was another long, empty silence, then Dad spoke again. "I'm turning in. You coming?"

꒰

I lay in bed a long, long time, needing to sleep, but not able to. Did other families have these hidden-away places full of sorrow? How was it that my parents carried such despair between them, while they went to work and came home and went to sleep at night in the same bed? Did Stargazer's family have secrets that were forbidden, locked away, never spoken of? Did all families?

Then something happens, like finding the ammo box, and the walled-off place cracks open and everything tumbles out.

I couldn't help but think about the hard hurt place in me where my friendship with Stargazer used to be. I burrowed deeper in my covers, trying to push away the cutting words that had flown between us, back to Beldon, back to baby killer.

But how could my dad, who felt so afraid when he couldn't remember what touching my mother felt like, how could he kill babies?

Vietnam, Spring 1975

Waves of pain tore through me like shrapnel. They started in my shoulder and ran down to my heart. I had my fingers stuffed in my mouth, holding back a word—Mà—that had already flown out. Fingers that held a photo that should have stayed hidden.

A wet rag rubbed my cheek, slid down my neck, and pulled off. A splashing in water, then the rag was back, wiping my neck.

Someone gently took my fingers out of my mouth, and I tasted salty blood. The rag washed my fingers, one at a time. I opened my eyes. A woman was sitting next to me, with a bowl of water, rusty brown with my blood.

"I'm Sister Phan Theresa," she said. "You're in the Lord's hands now. You are safe here."

I watched from under a tree by the fence outside Jones Brothers until I saw my chance. I could see Dad on the far side of the yard, filling an order in the forklift, a carpenter standing by his truck waiting. There were no customers inside the store. I slipped in and went straight up to Mr. Conner.

"Hi there, Monk—," he said. He cleared his throat. "Hi, Tracy," he said. Maybe he picked up the habit of giving people nicknames after being in the army.

"Can I ask you something?" I asked. Since he was a vet like my dad, I figured he could help me.

He looked surprised. "Sure."

"Alone?"

"Okay." He glanced over his shoulder at the open office door behind him. "Jones isn't in his office. How 'bout there?"

On the wall behind Mr. Jones's desk was a row of photos showing members of the local hunting club. One was a photo of Jimmie Jones, grinning, sitting on a four-point buck he'd shot.

Mr. Conner sat down in Mr. Jones's chair. I shut the door behind us and got right to it.

"Is my dad a baby killer?" I asked.

His eyebrows flew up. "Who said that?"

"Beldon."

"Uh-huh," he said, and crossed his arms over his chest. "Figures. Lemme explain something. When you're a soldier, you're just out there trying to stay alive. Sometimes crappy things happen, and they happen fast. In a war you do unforgivable things, things you're too young to understand. But I can promise you, your dad never killed any babies."

"How do you know?" My hands were jammed into such tight fists my nails were biting into my palms.

"Sweetheart, it's just what the hippies say." He slapped his open hand down on the desk. "They got no clue what goes on when you're out there fighting, protecting their freedom. But I promise you, nobody was going around sticking bayonets in babies, like they say."

Mr. Conner glanced at the office door, but he didn't move.

"Got any other questions for me?" he asked.

I pulled the chain over my head. The dogtag and key slid up my neck, caught in my hair. I pulled them out and handed the chain to him. He studied the dogtag silently, rubbed it with his thumb. "Let me see. I bet you found this at the same time as that ammo box you told me about."

I nodded.

"You know why you wear these things? In the shower, out in the field, when you think you're safe sitting on your bunk writing a letter home?"

He wasn't waiting for an answer. "It's so if you get killed, and your body is blown to bits, they know who you are. A dogtag says to you: every second could be your last."

He tossed the chain back to me. "I don't know why your dad had this. All I know is that ever since you found that ammo box, your dad's been a mess. Whatever you're up to, drop it, okay?"

Mr. Conner stood up. "I'm dead serious, Monkey." This time he didn't even remember to use my real name. "Jones called your dad in here a couple of days ago and told him to shape up, or he was out of a job."

He opened the door. There was my dad, staring straight at me. I pushed right past him.

꙳

Dad followed me out into the parking lot and whirled me around by the shoulder. "How dare you bring the dogtag in here." He held out his hand. I clenched my fist tight around the dogtag and shook my head.

"Who's James B. Kirby?" I asked.

He stared hard at me, shoved his hands in his pockets. "Rooster." There it was, plain and simple.

"Tell me," I said. "Please, you've got to tell me."

I could feel how much he didn't want to, didn't want to go near that place in him that hurt, didn't want to make words from the howling of the ghosts.

"You're acting like this was just your war," I said softly. "But it wasn't. It was my war too."

Dad looked at me for a minute, then nodded. "You're right.

"We called him Professor at first, because he always had his nose stuck in a book. He was a really sweet, quiet guy who'd do anything for his friends."

Dad stopped, swallowed, went on. "One night when I was on watch he came out to tell me all the lyrics to the new Beatles' song, 'Hey Jude.' He caught a sapper— a specially trained North Vietnamese soldier—under the concertina wire, heading for the bunkers. He yelled bloody murder he was so surprised, then tackled the guy with his bare hands."

Dad touched the side of his ribs. "The sapper got him right here with a knife. It was pretty bad, but he was patched up and back in a few weeks. That yell brought guys running, so instead of Professor we started calling him Rooster."

I wanted to ask where Rooster was now, like I did with Bluto, but I already knew the answer. He was dead. He was gone and my dad cried over him and trembled, and the ghosts howled around us.

"Did he die in Vietnam?" I whispered.

Dad nodded.

"He's the other guy, isn't he, with you and Bluto." Dad knew right away what I was talking about. He nodded again.

"How did he die?"

"Shot. A week before he was due to come home."

A week. He was short a week. Seven days. His ammo box, his dogtag.

"Were you with him?"

Dad spun on his heel, headed for his truck.

I ran after him, climbed into the passenger side just as he was putting the key in the ignition. "Wait, Dad. Please."

He let go of the key and dropped his hand into his lap. I undid the chain and pulled off the dogtag. "Here." I stuck it inside his curled-up fingers.

"I need to know," I said.

Dad nodded, stared straight ahead out the window.

"Okay. Yeah, okay," he said, like he was deciding something, getting his courage up.

"One morning a lieutenant told the three of us to run a quick perimeter check on a nearby village, show off our firepower. No shooting, just let 'em see what we were carrying. There'd been no trouble for weeks. We didn't even have a radio with us to call the QRF—quick reaction force—if we needed help."

The fingers of his empty hand drummed on the steering wheel. "It was a gorgeous day. Everything was so green. On the other side of the rice paddies women were weeding. It felt so . . . peaceful. We were walking on one of the rice paddy dikes. Puffy clouds in the sky, not hot yet. I was hanging back—" He broke off.

A big bluebottle fly trapped in the truck with us buzzed against the windshield.

"What happened?" I whispered.

"All hell broke loose." Dad swallowed. "There was a *clack-clack-clack*—one bamboo stick hitting another.

Like this . . ." He clapped three times. The sound bounced against the metal ceiling and doors. "We never saw anyone, bullets just started spraying from the tree line.

"I should have realized. It was too quiet. No birds were calling in the jungle. The women were silent, bent over. They never looked up at us as we walked in. They must have known we were walking into a trap."

Dad rubbed his eyes with the heels of his hands, like he could blot out what he was seeing. "Rooster was a city kid. Probably the greenest thing he ever saw before Vietnam was a baseball field."

The fly buzzed over to Dad's side and banged against his window, searching for an opening.

"I've replayed that moment in my head thousands of times. I've scanned the jungle, looking for a leaf that moved when there was no wind, listening for the sound of someone belly crawling . . ." His voice was so quiet now, I could barely hear him. "But it always comes out the same. Bluto and Rooster were both hit. They were lying in the sun, begging for help, for water, for morphine, and I couldn't reach them. They were too far away. Rooster was asking for his mama, talking about how he was supposed to see her soon."

Dad rolled the window down a few inches. The fly crawled up the glass and flew out.

"By the time it was dark and I could get to them, Rooster was dead."

He rolled the window back up. "I had let Rooster walk point. Just that once. He'd wanted to say he'd done it before he went home."

Dad opened his hand, stared at the dogtag.

"I was hanging in the back, writing a poem in my mind."

He looked at me for the first time. "There's one other thing you should know." He handed me the dogtag. "Rooster was your father."

Vietnam, Spring 1975

I wrapped my hands tight around the metal bars of the orphanage gate and stared out at the street. Schoolboys in blue shorts and white shirts rode by on their bikes, talking and laughing. Mopeds roared by, women pulled carts full of fruits and vegetables and live chickens to the Da Nang market. The whole world was streaming by the orphanage.

An old woman shuffled up to the stump outside the fence. She pulled matches and incense from the pocket of her overblouse. She lit the incense and pushed the smoking sticks into the stump. I could see her lips moving, knew she was muttering prayers for the forsaken spirits. I leaned my forehead against my fists and closed my eyes.

Grandmother used to pray at an old banyan tree outside the village for the forsaken spirits. Now I was lost, one of the forsaken spirits myself.

Elizabeth Partridge

We drove out of the yard. I left my bike, and Dad left work without saying anything to anyone. *Rooster-was-your-father.* It was like someone drumming out a rhythm on my head. The words didn't make sense, just the beat. *Rooster-was-your-father. Rooster-was-your-father.*

When Dad pulled into our driveway, I didn't go inside with him. Instead I told him I was going for a walk. He looked relieved. He probably wanted to be alone as much as I did. I headed straight up the hill behind our house. I climbed through the tall, dry oat grass and patches of slippery shale until I was up at the ridge road. I turned north, and walked along the edge of the asphalt until I came to a wide turnout.

There it all was, spread out below me. My house, tucked into the dry, grassy hills. Farther down I could see dozens of little buildings perched right on the edge of the ocean. I could make out the parking lot and flat roof of Redwood Cove Market, where Mom was working. Up past Jones Brothers, the north fork of the river made lazy, silvery twists, then widened out and dumped into the ocean. Tucked in a bend of the river I could just see Stargazer's trailer, and the tidy rows of his family's garden. Higher up was the deep, wide part of the river where we swam and hunted crayfish, and above that, the dark green of the redwood forest.

I looked back at Stargazer's property. He was probably there, along with Ruthie and Summer. Soon the new baby would be there too. A baby that belonged with her mother, her father, sister, and brother. A baby who would stay, and not be sent an ocean away.

I kicked a stone and watched it tumble down the hill, loosening a shower of pebbles that skittered and clattered down after it.

And me? I belonged to James B. Kirby. Rooster. A dead man.

～

For the rest of that day and the next, I avoided my parents. Under my face that showed nothing, I felt steely hard and cold. Dad had known all this time Rooster was my father and he'd never told me. What else did he know? Did he know about my grandmother with her rough, calloused hands that smelled of smoked fish, or if my mother was a prostitute? Did he know the nuns in the orphanage, and how all our bellies growled with hunger?

Dad must not have told Mom we talked, because

she didn't ask me anything. I stayed home and I read. I read anything short and meaningless—the advertising circular from Redwood Cove Market, the tiny print on the toothpaste tube. I read just to run words through my mind, words that went around and around and didn't say anything.

But when I put down the toothpaste, or walked out in the backyard to check again for a note, a thought kept swimming up.

I wanted to see Stargazer. He'd know how to figure this out. Stargazer with his lists, trying to hold away terrible things. Stargazer, who knew everything and could arrange words and put everything in order.

∽

Stargazer didn't leave me any more notes. But if I were to write him a note right now, I would make him a list of things he doesn't know about me:

1) James B. Kirby, also known as Rooster, is my father. My blood father.
2) My blood mother—Má—was very brave. She had strong arms and a strong heart.

3) Tracy is not my real name. My real name
   sounds like the cry of the shorebirds.

I touched my scar, and I thought about what Mr.
Conner had said.

"In a war you do unforgivable things, things you're
too young to understand."

Maybe someday I will tell Mr. Conner: I was never
too young to understand.

Vietnam, Spring 1975

The boys outside the gates didn't ride by on their bikes coming and going from school anymore. The street was filled with people from the countryside carrying bundles in their arms, or heaped in baskets that swung on long bamboo poles across their shoulders. Gunshots crackled, sometimes far away, sometimes near.

"North Vietnamese troops are coming," went from mouth to mouth. "Run."

They ran. Some in one direction, some the other.

In the orphanage, we had only one small handful of rice each day. At first the little ones cried, but after a few more days they were silent, sitting on their beds and in the courtyard with empty eyes.

At night we slept on the pews in the church, where Sister Theresa said Jesus would protect us. When the ground shook and trembled with rocket fire, Father Hue said the rosary, over and over again.

I didn't trust myself to stay awake if I got in bed, so I sat on my bedspread and watched the second hand on the clock sweep around and around. At eleven o'clock I slipped out the back door.

Outside, moonlight flooded everything. The night air was warm against my arms and legs as I coasted down the hill on my bike. On Highway One a tiny chill of fog hung in the air. I was prepared to pull off the road and hide in the bushes, but no cars came by the whole time. At Jones Brothers I turned and rode up the hill toward Stargazer's. But instead of going up his driveway, I rode uphill for another few minutes, then leaned my bike against the fencing, and cut through the neighbor's orchard, cleared long ago from the redwood forest.

I stopped at the crest of a hill under an apple tree and looked down at the river. It shone silver in the moonlight. I could see the rocks we liked to lie on, and the path from Stargazer's house. The only place the moonlight didn't reach were the redwoods. They looked dense, impenetrable. I trotted down to the rocks below.

I sat on the rocks and waited. It felt like I waited a

long time, long past midnight, but finally I saw Star-gazer on the path, pulling his wagon with the ship loaded on it.

"Almost there," he said. At first I thought he was talking to me, but then I saw a smaller, pale shape drift-ing behind him. It was Summer, in her nightgown.

She said something I didn't hear.

"If you hadn't dropped the flashlight and broken it," Stargazer said, "we'd be able to see better. Anyway, it's lucky the moonlight is so bright."

I stood up and called Stargazer's name.

He stopped.

"Go!" said Summer from behind him.

"It's me," I said.

"Tracy?"

Hearing his voice made me feel completely shy and unsure of myself. "I got your notes," I said.

Everything seemed to stand still, then Summer said, "Who's that?" like it was perfectly ordinary to run into someone out walking by the river in the middle of the night.

"It's me," I said.

"Good," said Summer.

"Yes," Stargazer said. "Good." But even in the

moonlight I could see him hesitate, uncertain what to do or say next.

"I said 'go!' " Summer repeated from behind Stargazer.

"Well?" I said. "What are we all waiting for?"

"Nothing," Stargazer said. He leaned forward and pulled, and the wagon started toward me. I ran to meet them. And I knew, just like that, Stargazer and I were friends again.

ॐ

We unloaded the ship by standing on either side and picking it up by the logs on the bottom. We set it with the front prow in the water and the back half on the rock, so we could shove it quickly into the river as soon as we lit it on fire. Stargazer had done a great job finishing the boat without me. He'd used a dowel for the mast, and hand-sewn a sail to it. He'd found some sheet metal and cut round shields and attached four of them to each side. Most beautiful of all was the dragon's head, perched on a long, curved neck.

I put my hand on top, right between the ears. It felt just like Pixie's wide head. Even the sharp teeth weren't so frightening. It seemed more like a happy, panting dog than a dragon. I was glad.

I gave it a pat, then asked, "Do Beldon and Ruthie know you're here?"

Stargazer shook his head. "No. But Jip and Pixie almost blew my cover, trying to follow us. And then it took forever to get here with Summer."

Stargazer didn't ask about my parents. He knew they wouldn't have let me come. "Why did you bring her?" I realized I was whispering.

"She woke up when I got out of bed. I had to."

Behind me, I heard Summer splash into the water. I turned around and she was standing up to her knees, bending over with her face close to the water.

"What're you doing?" Stargazer said. He waded in and grabbed her by the arm.

"Lapping water," she said. "I'm a baby bunny."

Stargazer pulled her back onto the flat rocks. "Remember what I said? You have to be really, really good to watch the Viking funeral ship burn up."

"I am good," she said.

"Listen," I said. "You have to watch us from right here, sitting on the rocks. We can't worry about you in the water."

Summer shook her arm free of Stargazer's grip.

"Sit down." Stargazer squatted on the rocks a little farther from the water. "Here's your nest."

"It's not soft," she said.

"Promise us you won't go near the water again," I said.

"Why?" she asked.

"Baby bunnies can't swim," I said quickly.

"Promise," Stargazer said, or I'm taking you home right now." He pulled off his T-shirt. "Here," he said. "To make your nest soft, little bunny."

"Okay," Summer said. "I promise."

He got her settled and we walked back over to the ship.

"Kinda too bad we have to burn it," I said.

"That's the whole point," he said. "Let's make everything perfect for the Viking king." He straightened the mast that had tipped sideways when we moved the ship. "When this sail burns, it's going to be spectacular," he said.

A chill wind blew up the river, and tendrils of fog drifted in front of the moon.

"What did you put in here to burn?" I asked him.

"Mostly dry pine needles. But I was afraid they

wouldn't last long enough to burn up the whole ship, so I put in some twigs, and then some little branches."

I glanced up at the moon. "We'd better hurry. We won't be able to see anything if the fog gets too thick."

Stargazer pulled a box of matches out of his pocket. "Strike Anywhere matches," he said.

A puff of wind blew out the first match as soon as he scraped it across one of the shields. Stargazer crouched down. "That wind is picking up fast," he said. I squatted next to him, and cupped my hands around his.

The next few matches died out right away, despite my help. The wind blew across the back of my neck and made me shiver. Behind us Summer was talking to herself about her soft nest and hunting owls.

Finally we figured out that the best way was to hold the matchbox inside the ship and strike the match on the box. The second time the flame stayed lit. Stargazer held it under the pine needles. "Come on, baby," he said.

With a sudden tiny rush, the flames crackled up through the needles. Stargazer fed twigs into the fire until it roared and snapped and popped. I stood back.

"Okay," Stargazer said, "time to launch." He hoisted up the back end of the ship and slid it into the water. Shreds of cold fog blew around us.

Stargazer kept walking until he was out in the water up to his waist. "That's far enough!" I called out. He gave the boat a final push just as the sail caught fire. He ran back through the water and stood next to me, dripping.

It was as beautiful as Stargazer had promised it would be. Red and yellow flames leaped above the mast. The shields gleamed in the firelight, then suddenly all the flames merged and the whole ship was blazing.

The ship listed, caught in the whirlpool near the far bank, just past the deep crayfish hole. It spun in a circle, picking up speed, going around faster and faster. Suddenly it shot out of the whirlpool and headed downstream toward the ocean.

We ran along the river as it curved first one way and then the other. We could hear the roar of the ocean, just around one more bend.

"Not much longer now," Stargazer crowed. He was right. The ship slid sideways, tipped over, and disappeared into the water with a hiss and a cloud of smoke and steam.

⌣

We thought of Summer at the exact same moment. I looked at Stargazer and wondered, *Do I look as scared as he does?* Then without saying a thing, we ran back to where we'd launched the ship and ran onto the rocks. "Summer," Stargazer called, his voice tight and quavery.

"Summer, where are you?" I called.

"Maybe she went back," Stargazer said, and looked over his shoulder at the path home. But he didn't sound convinced.

"Summer." He cupped his hands around his mouth and called her name, listened, then called again.

I had a terrible, terrible thought: *Please don't let this be the bad thing Stargazer was making lists about.*

"Listen, Stargazer," I said. "First we have to check the water. Just in case." I pushed away the images crowding in my mind. "I'll go upstream, you go down. Look on the edge, look in the water . . . She can't have gone far." I couldn't say any more, just turned and started walking fast up the river, calling her name.

A few minutes later we met back on the rocks, and stood next to her empty T-shirt nest.

"She went home. I just bet she went back to the trailer," Stargazer said. His teeth were chattering together so hard he could barely talk. I didn't know if it was because he was cold, or afraid. Probably both.

"You go home," I said. "Watch for her on the path,

call for her. If you don't find her, Beldon and Ruthie will know what to do."

Stargazer's breath came in little wheezy gasps.

"I'm going to keep looking here by the river," I said.

"Okay," said Stargazer. "Okay." But he didn't move.

I reached down, grabbed his T-shirt, and threw it at him. "Go!" I said, sounding just like Summer.

Stargazer turned and ran, like a deer from a hunter. After a few yards he slowed down, pulled on his T-shirt, and called her name.

In a few more yards he disappeared into a swirl of fog. I listened to his voice getting farther and farther away until I couldn't hear him anymore.

I forced myself to stop imagining Summer caught by the river, the current sweeping her down to where the cold ocean waves roared in and slid out, dragging pebbles and dreams and drowned little girls into the vast, heartless depths.

I made myself think of the land, of the rocks under my feet, the trees around me. Where would she have gone? Hopefully she went home. But maybe not. When had we seen her last? When Stargazer settled her down on his T-shirt. And while we were lighting the ship, she was still in her nest, talking about owls who ate baby bunnies.

And then we'd run down along the river. Without thinking of her. We'd left her alone, unprotected. She'd want to hide somewhere the owls couldn't find her. Was that back in her own bed? Or somewhere else?

Somewhere else would be under the trees, where bunnies hid from owls. She wouldn't go into the forest far, just far enough to be safe.

Vietnam, Spring 1975

Outside the gates people ran only one way now: to the water. To the American ships moored in the harbor, hoping to escape. I knew what the sisters whispered to one another: they've heard the Vietcong will kill everyone with the face of the enemy.

I found Summer in the redwood forest, curled up in the hollow left eons ago by an ancient redwood stump. I would have stumbled right past her, but when I stepped near her, she whimpered, just once. When I looked closely, I could see her nightgown made a pale glow on the dark forest floor.

"Summer?" I squatted down.

"Cold," she said.

I put my hand out, found her arm. She was very cold.

"It's scratchy," she said.

"Come on," I said. "Let's go back."

"No," she said. "Too cold."

"We'll get warm walking," I said. I rubbed her arm, trying to wake her up, to convince her she'd be warm soon.

She curled into a tighter ball.

Tiredness swept through me. I'd never be able to carry her all the way back.

I eased over her, tucked myself around her. The ground was soft with leaf litter, but she was right, it was incredibly scratchy. "It's cold and scratchy because you are such a little baby bunny you don't have any fur yet," I said.

She whimpered.

"I'll get you all warm," I said, "and then we'll go back."

Summer wriggled closer to me, and I heard the wet sound of her sucking her thumb.

∿

The ghosts came to visit me.

Rooster came first, carrying his ammo box close to

his chest, a dark bullet hole right in the middle of his forehead. His dogtag tapped out a rhythm against the box with every step he took. He smelled of mud, and open cans of evaporated milk, and death.

Grandmother glided by in her canoe, her long oars surging forward to dip into the water. She leaned into the oars, disappeared behind the trees and reappeared, her bones glued together with grit and sorrow. I blinked, and she and the boat were gone.

Má stood nearby, with her soft shorebird cry, "Too-et, Too-et." Even in the dark, I could see her bright eyes, full of a kind of shocked disbelief, and longing so thick I could practically touch it.

There was the ghost of Dad, sitting against a tree near us. Young Bob pinned down by bullets. Bob, who made it over to Rooster too late. Bob, who tattooed Rooster on his back so he could carry him until his own skin shriveled and turned to dust in his grave.

The last echoes of Má's shorebird cry faded away as dawn turned the sky a rosy gray.

Dad's ghost stayed.

As light filtered into the forest I saw his hands tremble.

Then I understood. Dad had found me and was

waiting. Waiting for me to forgive him for all of the things he couldn't say, for hiding inside himself, for wrapping his skin tight around his unhappy heart every day before climbing, once more, out of bed. To forgive him what he could not forgive himself.

I opened my mouth to speak, felt how dry my mouth was. "How did you find us?" I asked.

Dad shifted, and the redwood leaf litter crackled under him.

"Chickadee, I walked point for a year in Nam. You were easy." Dad laughed quietly. " 'Course, that last note Stargazer left you gave me a pretty good heads-up. When I woke up in the middle of the night and you weren't in your bed—hadn't even *been* to bed—I knew where to start looking."

"Are you sorry?" I asked. He knew right away what I meant. Not walking point. Not Vietnam. Not betraying Rooster. We both knew he was sorry about all of that.

"I mean me. Me being here." I just had to say it, out loud.

Silence stretched between us. Then he cleared his throat.

"I claim you, Tracy," he said. "I will always claim you."

It was fiercer than just plain love. And somehow it snuck into that huge emptiness inside me and sat right there in my scooped-out place like a little red bean, and I figured with some time, it would probably be enough to fill me up.

Vietnam, Spring 1975

"Get up," said Sister, shaking my shoulder. "They have come for you."

I leaped to my feet, my heart hammering in my ears. Who had come for me?

Sister grabbed me by the hand, pulled me from the room.

Two Americans were waiting for me in the courtyard. Outside the open gates of the orphanage another man sat in the jeep. When he saw us he honked impatiently.

Even in the early morning light, people were rushing toward the water, parting to go around the jeep, then coming together again. The street was covered with discarded bundles of clothes, boxes, baskets, carts. Somewhere a child screamed, a man's voice called back, rough and full of fear.

Sister handed some papers to one of the GIs, pushed me toward the jeep. "Hurry," she said, "and may Jesus protect us all."

Dad was carrying Summer when we met the hunting club. We were heading up the path from the river and they were coming down. The whole club had turned out to search for us, carrying blankets and thermoses, flares and guns. Mr. Conner was leading the way, nearly running on his bandy cowboy legs to stay in front. Even Jimmie Jones was there with his hunting rifle, right behind Mr. Conner.

When they saw us, they stopped and cheered, and Beldon ran toward us. Jimmie raised his rifle like he was going to fire an announcing shot into the air, but Mr. Conner swung his arm back to stop him.

Dad handed Summer to Beldon, and Mr. Conner threw a blanket around them both. Somebody else wrapped another blanket around my shoulders.

჻

Dad surprised me the next morning at breakfast. Mom had made scrambled eggs and we'd just finished eating. "You still want to see the ammo box?" he said.

I couldn't believe he'd had it all this time. "Where is it?"

"In my toolbox, on the back of the truck."

Rooster's ammo box. With his crossed-out numbers, the silent footsteps of his fate coming to get him. But for the first time when I thought of the ammo box, I didn't feel the ghosts pressing in on me.

"Maybe later," I said.

"There's one other thing you didn't find," he said. He got up from the table and brought over the coffee-pot, refilling Mom's cup and then his.

"What?" I asked.

"What are you two talking about?" Mom asked.

Dad left the room and came back with the pink photo album.

He opened the album out flat, pulled back the cover, and shook. A black-and-white photo fell out.

He handed it to me. "This was pinned on your shirt when you arrived."

It was me, about the same age as I was in the first picture in my baby book. I was standing on a cracked tile floor, holding a small sign in both my hands. Behind me was a long, empty table with benches on either side. The orphanage.

"Bob, what are you doing?" Mom said.

"It's okay," he said.

"But we agreed . . . it would be best not to say anything."

I looked at Mom. Tears welled up in her eyes. She slid to the front of her chair like she was going to get up.

Dad put a hand on her arm. "She needs to know."

Mom shook her head. "No, I . . ."

They were talking like I wasn't even there, sitting at the table with them.

Dad leaned closer to Mom. "We can't keep running, all of us. You asked me what happened." He made a big, hopeless gesture. "All this happened, to all of us."

Mom sat back, put her hand over her mouth like she was stopping herself from saying something.

I looked back at the picture. There were two tiny pinholes at the top. The sign had two lines of writing.

Tran, Tuyet
8 October 1968

Dad pointed to the sign, his finger trembling across the little letters. "Your name. Your last name was Tran. And of course, your birthday."

I'd been labeled too, just like James B. Kirby. Not for my blood type, but to make sure I made it from *there* to *here*. Right here, to this place on the globe, to this family, to this table.

Tu-yet. It wasn't just the call of the shorebirds. I spelled out the letters softly to myself. My mother had named me Tuyet.

"Was she a prostitute?" I asked Dad.

"Who?" he said, confused.

"My blood mother."

"What gave you that idea?" he said. "Rooster was crazy in love with her. They met on the base."

"But they weren't married."

"No," Dad said.

"I thought when you loved somebody, you got married."

Dad cleared his throat, glanced at Mom. She shrugged, gave him a "see what you started" look.

"Rooster was already married. He had a wife and kid back here. But he planned to take care of you. Both of you."

I pulled out the dogtag, rubbed my fingers over the letters. Somewhere Rooster had a son or daughter who was rightfully his, with his last name. For a second that felt bad, but then I thought: *neither of us has him.*

I slipped the dogtag back in my shirt. "How'd you find me?" I asked Dad. "I mean, the first time in Vietnam."

"Grandee, believe it or not. She knew Henry Kissinger through the State Department."

"Who's that?"

"He was Secretary of State. A guy with a lot of power, believe me."

"Did he come get me?"

"Nah," said Dad. "Just shook the military command, top to bottom. Some top brass in Da Nang tracked you down somehow. You ended up getting thrown onto one of the last flights out, with a bunch of other orphans.

"Your mom and I had just about given up when we got a call you were at the airport."

I looked over at Mom again. She was slumped down in her chair, staring at the table. She must have felt me looking at her, because she glanced up, and I could see her hand, still tight over her mouth, was wet with tears.

She pulled her hand away, wiped tears off her face with her sleeve in one long un-Mom-like move.

"It's okay, Mom," I said. "I do want to know."

Mom shook her head slightly, blew her nose on her napkin. "I just don't want to lose you," she whispered. "I'm afraid . . ."

I didn't know how to say that right now, from this minute on, she had me more than she ever had. "It's okay," I said again. "Really."

Dad let out a big breath. "Well," he said loudly. "Phew!"

I started laughing, and Dad did too. Even Mom almost managed to smile.

I still had a lot more questions. But I didn't think I could take any more answers right now. Besides, I figured there was plenty of time to ask them.

"Can I go over to Stargazer's?" I asked. "He says he wants to build a replica of the Kon-Tiki next."

"Only if you promise—," Mom said, but I jumped to my feet and interrupted her.

"I know, I know. We won't launch it without you and Dad, okay?"

"It's a deal," she said with a shaky smile.

♫

Stargazer and I didn't get very far on the Kon-Tiki raft. We kept saying we were going to work on it, but we just didn't. Most afternoons we went swimming in the river, and we hung out a lot with Summer so Ruthie could take it easy. Sometimes we helped Beldon in the garden. Stargazer quit carrying his notebook around, which I figured was a really good sign that the rest of the summer would go well.

On August 15, Ruthie had her baby. It was a girl, just like she thought. A few days later, Beldon called a family meeting and said of course I was invited. Ruthie put the baby in the middle of the table and we all sat around her and tried to figure out what name fit her best. Summer wanted to name her Bunny, but luckily Ruthie didn't go for it.

She'd given up the Moon Dance idea too, and wanted to know what we thought of naming the baby Andrea, after her sister. We all stared at the baby for a while, and somehow Andrea seemed perfect, though I can't exactly say why.

Beldon picked her up, kissed her on the cheek, and said, "Welcome to your little spot in the big world, Andrea."

And it gave me only a tiny pang of jealousy.

The last day of summer vacation I told Stargazer instead of going swimming I wanted to take him to the beach. My beach. We rode our bikes over to the Redwood Cove Market and I led him down the skinny path. He was already wearing his backpack, like he was ready for school. We walked into the ocean and stood up to our knees in the water for a while and felt the sand and pebbles suck out from under our feet with the waves.

Right then I knew that the scooped-out place in me would never go away completely. It would always be inside me, an empty space that held the ghosts of Má and Grandmother, the smells of charcoal and fish and a tea-colored river. I'd always know Rooster loved my mother but couldn't marry her, and that Vietnam was where he died, and where Dad lost some part of himself.

We went higher up the beach and Stargazer shrugged off his backpack. We leaned up against a big redwood log and watched the shore birds run along the edge of the waves and cry, *too-et, too-et*.

Someday, when it wasn't all so tender in me, I'd show Stargazer the photo of me in the Vietnamese orphanage, the one tucked in my American baby book. I'd tell him about the pieces of me I was trying to knit together, how I was trying to forgive myself for everything that happened before and after the Boss Man put the tip of his knife to my neck and let me slide down, just a little.

Right now, it helped to feel the dogtag and my door key against my skin. Dad said I could keep the dogtag and wear it as long as I wanted to. "Forever, if you want," he'd said. I didn't think it would be forever. Just till that scooped-out place in me felt stronger.

Stargazer threw a handful of pebbles toward the ocean. "You ready for school, Tracy?" he asked.

"Not Tracy," I said.

"Huh?" he said.

"My name is Tuyet," I said. "My real name."

"Really?" said Stargazer.

I nodded.

Stargazer reached into his backpack and pulled out one of his new notebooks. Suddenly I was worried. Did he think junior high was going to be so bad that he needed to start one of his lists?

"It's okay," he said. "I'm just getting a jump on that essay they always make us write at the beginning of school."

He opened his notebook to the first page, wrote something, and then said, "Spell it."

"Spell what?" I asked.

"Your real name."

"T-u-y-e-t," I said. "But you don't say the y. It sounds like those shorebirds," I said, pointing to them.

He wrote something else and passed the notebook to me.

<u>What I Did This Summer</u> (in reverse order)
by Stargazer
   1) I learned my best friend's name is Tuyet.
It sounds just like the call of the plovers.

"Those are plovers?" I asked, and pointed at the shorebirds running back and forth.

"Yep," said Stargazer.

"You know," I said, "you're going to run out of new things to learn by the time you are old, like fifty. And you'll be bored to death the rest of your life."

"Never," he said.

We sat in the sun with our eyes closed and listened to the plovers as they chased in and out of the water. For a long time, neither of us said anything. We let the last day of summer just stretch out between us and the horizon.

After awhile I realized I still had something to ask Stargazer, but I was having a hard time saying it. But if I couldn't start with Stargazer, I wasn't going to be able to do it at all.

Stargazer nudged me on the shoulder. "What?" he said.

I opened my eyes. He was looking right at me, waiting.

"Will you call me Tuyet?" I said.

Stargazer grinned. "Sure." He threw out his arms. "Welcome to your little spot in the big world, Tuyet."

Appendix

Is Tracy/Tuyet based on a real person? How about Stargazer and the other people in the book?
None of them are based on any one person. *Dogtag Summer* is historical fiction, meaning I took a slice of history that was very real (historical), and put in people from my imagination (fiction). I started the novel by doing a lot of reading and interviewing people in America and Vietnam who had lived through the war. This helped me understand what life was like for ordinary people caught up in a huge political and military conflict they had no control over.

There are two real people mentioned in the book. Walter Cronkite, anchor for CBS news from 1962 to 1981, gave nightly reports on the war. Henry Kissinger was the US National Security Advisor and later Secretary of State from 1973–1977, playing a huge role in our military decisions in Vietnam.

Sometimes I took real incidents and wove them into the novel. One Vietnamese adoptee, Dan Brown, told me how his adoptive American father, desperate to get him out of a Vietnamese orphanage after several years of red tape, finally called Secretary Kissinger and asked for help. Kissinger sent an aide to fly Dan to the United States. Unusual? Extremely. But did it really happen? Yes. This is why people say "truth is stranger than fiction."

Why did we send our troops to fight and die in Vietnam, a small country far away from us? And who were we fighting?
In 1954, Vietnam was divided in the middle at the 17th parallel. North Vietnam had a communist government; South Vietnam was a democracy. Americans fought on the side of the South Vietnamese Army, also known as the Army of the Republic of Vietnam (ARVN). We were fighting against the communist North Vietnamese Army (NVA), also known as the People's Army of Vietnam (PAVN).

How do the Vietcong figure in this?
They were affiliated with the communists and had both regular and guerilla units. The guerillas—farmers by day, and fighters by night—didn't wear uniforms, and it was almost impossible for the Americans to tell who was Vietcong and who was civilian.

Vietnam has a long history of being invaded and ruled by foreign countries, primarily China, as well as France and Japan. The United States sent in troops, conducted massive bombing raids, dropped napalm, and sprayed Agent Orange. Understandably, the Vietnamese called this new invasion the "American War."

Why did we fight this war in the first place?

This was the time of the Cold War. In America, we were afraid that if Communism spread from China down through all of Vietnam, it would have a domino effect. First one, then another Southeast Asian country would fall to Communism. President Kennedy sent hundreds of military advisors to South Vietnam. President Johnson escalated the war heavily, repeatedly sending in more troops and ordering more bombing raids. By the end of 1965, nearly eighty thousand American troops were in Vietnam. By 1969, we had more than half a million troops serving in Vietnam. The war continued under President Nixon, and it finally ended during Gerald Ford's presidency.

Which side were people like Tuyet's grandmother on?

That's hard to say. Her children fought on both sides, pulled by different forces. Like many villagers, her primary goal was just to stay alive. For survival, she had to appear to be on the side of whoever was in power in her village or hamlet. In many villages, the South Vietnamese and Americans were "in charge" during the day. The Vietcong would infiltrate at night, insisting on loyalty to the North. Sometimes they demanded food or medicine, and other times they punished or killed those who sided with the Americans.

Vietnamese women were an essential part of the conflict. With many of the men gone, they learned to plow the rice paddies and run the large irrigation pumps. Some smuggled weapons, food, and medicine for the Vietcong, and occasionally even fought alongside the men. Other women worked on American bases. They cleaned up the barracks, shined GIs' boots, and worked in the laundries. Some worked in bars and nightclubs in the cities, and some were prostitutes.

So that meant babies, right?

Right. Thousands of children of American servicemen and Vietnamese women were born during the war—some estimates are as high as one hundred thousand. These kids were known as *con lai*, half-breed, or *bui doi*, children of the dust. Scorned by the Vietnamese, almost all of them had really tough lives.

There were hundreds of small orphanages throughout Vietnam, filled with kids who were orphaned, were separated from their parents, or had parents who couldn't care for them. Usually these orphanages were run by Catholic and Buddhist nuns. They dedicated their lives to caring for the children, but there were always too many kids, too little medical care, and not enough food. Some American GIs tried to help, bringing food and clothing, providing basic medical care, and fixing buildings.

Did many of the Amerasian orphans know their fathers?
Tuyet's story is unusual. Very few soldiers took responsibility for their children. Some had no idea they'd fathered a child. If a man did know he'd gotten a woman pregnant, chances are he went back to America before the baby was born, or soon afterward. Some GIs fell in love with Vietnamese women, but the military actively discouraged GIs from marrying Vietnamese women.

Which country lost more lives—Vietnam or America?
Overwhelmingly, Vietnam. Around four million Vietnamese died, most of them civilians. Over fifty-eight thousand Americans died. A staggering number of them were teenagers—the average age of the American GIs in Vietnam was only nineteen.

Did they want to serve in the armed forces and go fight in Vietnam?
Some young men felt it was their patriotic duty, but not everyone wanted to go. During the Vietnam War, we

had a draft until 1973. All men between the ages of eighteen and twenty-five were required to register with the Selective Service, and every year thousands were drafted from this pool. Until 1971, when the voting age was lowered from twenty-one to eighteen, many soldiers were not old enough to vote. They were considered too young to vote, in many states they were too young to drink, but they weren't too young to fight and die for their country.

Whether they wanted to go or not, they were greeted as war heros when they came home, right?
Not usually. The United States was deeply divided in a way we hadn't been since the Civil War. Starting in the late sixties, there was an active antiwar movement in America, determined to get our military out of Vietnam. The television reporting of the war turned many people, like Stargazer's father, Beldon, against the war, angry at our government and the GIs who had fought there.

Many Vietnam vets felt isolated when they got home. They'd risked their lives for America, and instead of thanks, they were criticized. It was hard to talk about their experiences with people at home who had no understanding of what they'd gone through.

If the antiwar movement was for peace, why were the protestors so angry?

They didn't see the war as vital to our national security, and were frustrated at the continual death and destruction in Vietnam. Some of the targets of their anger were wrong, like blaming the soldiers who had fought in Vietnam.

One thing is really confusing. How could Tracy/Tuyet forget all about her life in Vietnam?

Today we understand much more about how post-traumatic stress disorder (PTSD) affects people. Tuyet lived in constant danger. She was kidnapped, hurt, and thrown into an orphanage. Without warning she was pulled out and flown to a different country. She lost people who loved her, her home, the foods she ate, the language she spoke, and even her name.

One way of coping with such massive trauma is to forget who you were and remember only your new life. But for PTSD sufferers, the past rarely is quiet, but can be triggered unexpectedly, as it was with Tuyet and Bob.

People with PTSD can have crippling nightmares, flashbacks, outbursts of anger, and trouble concentrating. Like Bob, some use unhealthy coping strategies like alcohol or drugs. War veterans often struggle alone with PTSD, feeling isolated, anxious, and ashamed they can't pull themselves together.

After the war, did the Vietcong really kill any of the con lai kids?

I don't know. But the rumor spread like wildfire. It was part of a terrible fear of retribution against anyone who had collaborated with the Americans and South Vietnamese.

In the last days before the communists took over, hundreds of Vietnamese "orphans" were hastily loaded on planes and sent to America to be adopted in Operation Babylift. Some caregivers made a special effort to get the mixed-blood children out of Vietnam. Later it turned out that not all of the Vietnamese kids were orphans, but were put on the planes by parents who believed they would join their children later in America.

Once the Americans left and the Communists took over, did things go smoothly for the Vietnamese?

Unfortunately, no. It was an unbelievably hard period of time for most Vietnamese. There were millions of refugees and hundreds of thousands of kids separated from their parents or orphaned. Around a million desperate people fled the country, many as "boat people." They risked their lives trying to escape, crowded in small, open boats in the ocean, with little water and food. We'll never know how many drowned, died of thirst or exposure, or were robbed and then killed by pirates.

After the war, the Communists took away private ownership of farms and factories. Around a million people suspected of collaborating with the South Vietnamese and Americans were sent to "reeducation camps." Many died of starvation and disease.

Thousands of children of GIs remained in Vietnam after the war. As they got older, some formed small packs in the cities and survived by begging, doing small jobs, scavenging, and stealing. They rarely were able to go to school.

Did all the GIs in Vietnam wear dogtags?

Yes. The military issued two metal dogtags to each GI, stamped with their name, social security or serial number, blood type, and religion. "NO PREF" was short for "no preferred religion." Some GIs wore both dogtags around their neck with black electrical tape or plastic "silencers" on the tags, or one tag on a short chain attached to the main chain around their neck. Others threaded one dogtag into a bootlace on their tough combat boots. If their body was blown apart in heavy combat, the dogtag on the boot had a better chance of being found.

Why are dogtags such a big deal?

When an American soldier is killed in combat, his body is recovered, if at all possible, and returned to the United States for burial. Along with his personal effects, his family is given the American flag that was draped over his coffin, as a symbol of the soldier's ultimate sacrifice for his country. For some grieving family members a dogtag can mean even more than the flag. It can be the last tangible link to their loved one.

Wait a sec. Why did Bob have Rooster's dogtag then? Shouldn't it have gone to his family?

Soldiers often kept their own mementos of fallen buddies—a favorite pack of cards, a photo, a hat, or a dogtag. Tucked away, these mementos were kept to remember, to grieve, and to honor.

Every year, veterans are among the four million visitors to the Vietnam Veterans Memorial in Washington DC. Along with flags and notes, some of these mementos are left at the Wall in a final tribute. www.thewall-usa.com.

Acknowledgments

Many generous people helped me with this book.

I am deeply thankful to Jim Iversen, whose memories of combat started me on this journey. He opened my eyes to the intense, conflicting pressures that American soldiers faced in the Vietnam War.

Thanks to my amazing editor, Melanie Cecka, whose guidance and encouragement were crucial, and my agent, Ken Wright, whose insight and advice was—and is—always right on.

There's no way to express my deep gratitude to the writers, colleagues, and friends who made the journey with me, reading the manuscript, sorting out wrong turns, and encouraging me through dark nights of the soul: Tom Birdseye, Judy Blundell, Donna Brooks, Clair Brown, Bruce Coville, Julie Downing, Jill Davis, Patti Gauch, Anna Grossnickle Hines and Gary Hines, Suzanne Johnson, Karen

Kashkin, Joan Lovett, Andrea Nachtigall, Rebecca Sherman, Katherine Tillotson, and Patty Whitman. A special shout-out to Susan Campbell Bartoletti, who pored over many drafts and always brought me back to the heart of the story.

My thanks to the dedicated, ever-patient librarians at the Berkeley Public Library and the University of California at Berkeley who found me books and old magazine articles and buried gems of information. And when it was time to stop researching and start writing, my refuge was an old, heavy table in the Anthropology Library in Kroeber Hall at UC Berkeley, where the librarians knew just when to stop offering me more materials and let me be.

For vivid details of her childhood in Vietnam I am indebted to Nga Trinh, and for showing me Vietnam today and sharing his experiences during and after the war, Quang Van Nguyen. Special appreciation to Mai Vu for her memories and for enlisting her mother's and Vietnamese grocer's aid in checking each detail in my manuscript.

There are both unique and universal issues with being adopted from one culture into another. I'm deeply grateful to those who shared their feelings and experiences of being adopted internationally, especially Dan Brown (previously named Tri Viet Nguyen) and Deann Borshay Liem. (She's made two incredible documentary films on her adoption and identity, *First Person Plural* and *In the Matter of Cha Jung Hee*.)

My thanks to Ron and Martha Berryman, who explained intricacies about the military and Vietnam that had eluded me, and to Donna Tauscher, for courageously sharing her memories of her ex-husband's Vietnam war service and how it changed him, their marriage, and the fabric of her life.

I'm grateful to my awesome, supportive family who tiptoed around me when I was cranky and preoccupied, and welcomed me back with open arms and home-cooked meals when I emerged from a writing session: sons Felix and Will Ratcliff, sisters Joan and Meg Partridge, and my dad, Rondal Partridge, with his laser-look and urgent question, "Tell me, how's the writing going?"

And most of all to my husband, Tom Ratcliff, always willing to listen and offer invaluable advice. His understanding of the complexity of politics, war, and human nature infuse every page of this book.

Elizabeth Partridge graduated with a degree in women's studies from the University of California, Berkeley, and later studied traditional Chinese medicine. She was an acupuncturist for more than twenty years before closing her medical practice to write full time.

Elizabeth is the acclaimed author of more than a dozen books for young readers, including *Marching for Freedom*, as well as biographies of Dorothea Lange, Woody Guthrie, and John Lennon. Her books have received many honors, including being a National Book Award finalist and winning the Boston Globe–Horn Book Award, the Los Angeles Times Book Prize, a Michael L. Printz Honor, and the Jane Addams Children's Book Award. Elizabeth lives with her family in Berkeley, California.

www.elizabethpartridge.com